D1235812

The Sign for Drowning

The Sign *for* Drowning

A Novel

RACHEL STOLZMAN

Trumpeter · *Boston* · 2008

Trumpeter Books
An imprint of Shambhala Publications, Inc.
Horticultural Hall
300 Massachusetts Avenue
Boston, Massachusetts 02115
www.shambhala.com

9 8 7 6 5 4 3 2 1

First Edition

Printed in the United States of America

♾ This edition is printed on acid-free paper that meets the
American National Standards Institute Z39.48 Standard.
Distributed in the United States by Random House, Inc.,
and in Canada by Random House of Canada Ltd

Library of Congress Cataloging-in-Publication Data

Stolzman, Rachel.
The sign for drowning: a novel / Rachel Stolzman.—1st ed.
p. cm.
ISBN 978-1-59030-587-4 (hardcover: alk. paper)
I. Title.
PS3619.T65635S54 2008
813'.6—dc22   2007041845

For my sister, Dana, who taught me to go far out

. . . the same day were all the fountains of the great deep broken up, and the windows of heaven were opened.

—Genesis 7:11

The Sign for Drowning

Prologue

My father and Carla towed the yellow inflatable boat carrying the girls into the water. The low tide held them far out, bobbing in the small waves. The girls were both five years old, born just a week apart, my mother and Carla having met in a birthing class. Every day my father took the girls out in the rubber raft, some days two or three times.

My father held the boat behind where Megan was sitting. Carla stood behind Bonnie. I know the inexplicable behavior of the sea—when the tide seems to push up against the shore and the undertow slips out like a fluid carpet toward the ocean's vast center and the whole sea heaves its chest.

When the waves fattened and heightened, Dad motioned Carla to push out farther, beyond the break. He guided the boat, seeking the solace of the rolling hills that the ocean offers anyone who can penetrate its crashing shoulder.

We were girls, with lungs, not gills. But I was in no danger. I stood in the dry sand, watching.

Megan wore a navy blue bathing suit with a sailboat on it. I remember her skinny arms and muscular legs, slow brown eyes and long lashes. She had a beauty mark on her right cheek and a matching one on her right buttock. I remember that.

My mother was on the shore with me, making a home

movie of the girls, Dad, and Carla playing in the big surf. I looked at Megan's and Bonnie's upturned faces, smiling expectantly at the down-crashing wave. I heard Megan squeal. My mother bumped into me with her camera. We both laughed at their predicament.

The wave came down without question or hesitation, unbidden, naturally. When the three of them surfaced, both Carla and Dad had their hands on Bonnie's streaming body. Surfacing, my father looked as ungraceful as a human out of his element. He threw his head back, cleared water from his blinking eyes. Carla was gasping. From the shore we noticed first; Megan was not in the boat.

For several long seconds after Megan vanished, with the camera's eye, my mother searched the surrounding water. She filmed until she realized that she was still holding the camera, realized that Megan was truly underwater too long.

It is obvious in my mother's movie that Megan is gone, as though the camera, the viewer, the audience, were omniscient. I was the first to fully realize that Megan was under the waves. I was watching Carla, her hands wrapped under Bonnie's arms, gripping her child's chest, looking to my father in disturbed confusion.

It was Carla's expression that finally alerted my father to Megan's absence. In our home movie you see his eyes frantically jump to his hands. It registers. He's holding Bonnie's small calves, not Megan's. Then he grabs for his own thighs, as if he might be on the warm beach, Megan safe in his lap. Now the camera starts scanning the surrounding waters. You can feel the panic in the rapid pacing of the churning waves. In actuality the ocean had calmed terrifically, as though satisfied.

Dad and Carla started clapping the water around their bodies. My father shouting, "But she can swim! She can swim!" The film heads into its epilogue of drifting sand. As my mother drops the camera, it turns lazily, falling downward, and there is a brief framing of the cloudless sky before the camera comes to rest. The film ends with many minutes of sand. It is not motionless; the wind is blowing grains in front of the lens.

One of Megan's and my favorite beach games was to stand at the tip of the shore, where each creeping wave could only lap around our toes and halfway up our heels. We loved the way the wet sand sucked at the bottoms of our feet. As my mother charged into the ocean, I was acutely aware of this sensation. I was immobile.

On the nape of my neck, fine hairs standing up, thin skin raised in bumps. The water looked too strong. Hands in fists, I dug my nails into my palms, drew my fingers up to my face. In the soft flesh below my eyes, I pressed my nails, making deep crescents. My sister was lost underneath. Burning juice rose from my stomach, scalded my throat. I was eight years old. I was afraid for her and for myself.

The guilt began immediately as I felt the ocean pull at my feet, the same way it pulled at my sister. I knew that I would not be able to move, that I would remain on the beach, mute and watchful. I believed at this time that if I stood perfectly still and did nothing but concentrate on Megan's appearing, I could will her back from whatever depth. It was then that I began speaking to Megan without words.

My mother beat the surface of that great body of water, as if enough force would cause it to relinquish her child. Megan did make contact, a final touch with Carla. This part I always omit when recounting Megan's death. It seems too cruel and impossible.

Suddenly Carla was yelling, "I've got her!" She glanced at Bonnie, who was holding the side of the raft. Carla peered into the opaque water, and dove under. We above shared an eager relief. Of course she's okay. This was only a terrible scare. Carla emerged, her face shattered, humility. She immediately dove again. My mother howled. Carla surfaced a minute later; Bonnie raised her arms toward her and whimpered. Carla moved back toward the boat. "She brushed against my leg." Then she clutched her own baby.

My parents began diving and surfacing, diving and surfacing. Carla held Bonnie, both crying and visibly shivering. It was then that I realized I was holding my breath. Good, of course; as long as I can hold my breath she's still alive! Then my last hope was not to breathe and to wait for Megan. I stood there bursting in my head and chest, knowing that Megan could not hold out this long. Racked with choking, I knew that I had failed. I stood breathing on the shore.

As my mother had seen through the camera's eye, I saw what was happening through Megan's eyes. With her eyes open, Megan knew which direction was the surface, was air. But she couldn't raise her body out of the gripping current while being tossed one way and another. She saw the surface. She saw the green-gray water and the sun coming through the water, illuminating particles. For a brief moment she saw Carla's pale leg, pivoting nervously. The current even forced her against this sturdy leg for a moment, and then tossed her back even farther. Her eyes never closed, she kept them open, focused on her life. I saw what she saw. And all the while, seeing the sun's rays, the sloshing surface, feeling the push and pull of the undertow, the salty water going down, there was silence. The silence lay heavy over all the sensations, heavy and calming. Her arms reached for us, cried out for us. She kept her mouth shut against the water. She motioned to the retreating figures of the boat, her father's legs, all of it, until she couldn't anymore and closed her eyes to the silence.

We remained there. The ocean moved back into its own low sleepful state.

It is the first ten minutes of searching that I grieve for, the searching that could have been of consequence. They searched for more than an hour without ceasing, and then again when the coast guard arrived. And then again, my father went out uncontrollably in the early dawn, where he roared about like an elephant seal in vain pursuit.

The following day, in the backseat of the car, fleeing the Cape, back into the body of Massachusetts, I understood without doubt: Had I entered the ocean and physically searched, I would have saved her. Her body would have been magnetically attracted to mine. But by then it was useless.

My mother would later plead, "Why did I hold the camera so long?" We all thought we'd done the wrong thing, could have saved her. It was incredibly hard to realize she was drowning. It would have been easier to believe that she was flying above the boat than not breathing beneath it. We have not destroyed the film, because of the insane hope; it's the one possibility of still finding her. We could still search the black-and-white water, for a hand or a small head surfacing.

My father took the girls out in the boat each day, sometimes several times in a day. Even at dusk, when my mom complained that it was too dark. The morning Megan drowned was very bright, and no one was thinking of danger. There is no reason that Megan drowned instead of Carla's large daughter, Bonnie. I often wished it had been reversed. I have always thought that the ocean had to swallow some child that day.

BOOK ONE

———— ⊙ ————

We have been reading *The Little Prince*. Not the usual image of a mother reading to a child. We face each other. She watches my eyes and my hands. Adrea is deaf as a stone. Adrea says that I named her.

Our first contact was a spring day in her classroom at the Huntington School. I frowned at the stained rug, ripped books, bare barred windows. Frowned at the eight special foster children. Her rounded tense back suddenly curled against my shins. She was sitting on my feet, facing away, holding herself. An introduction.

I looked down at this unfamiliar five-year-old child, her head resting against my knees. Her hair was neatly parted down the middle, braids curving down each side like rivers rushing to reach the back of her neck. Lowering myself to the floor, I was careful to keep my legs steady and not jostle the girl. She spun around, placing her small feet on top of mine. She wrapped her arms around her knees, looked directly at my face and then away. I read her name tag and signed, "Hello, Adrea."

She pursed her lips tentatively, broke into a smile. Two rows of perfect baby teeth. Slowly she brought out one grubby hand, signed carefully, "My name is —" then in a rush, "Adrea," as I had.

I had skipped a letter, a loose fist, two fingers over the thumb, two fingers under the thumb—N. We'd made a truce, unknowingly, that would be permanent.

I put aside the book. We need to talk about a flower that loves. Adrea wants to know what I believe. God, I need to know her every belief. We agree a flower can love; so can a plant and a tree. Lying on Adrea's bed, the sun boasting and rain tapping down, hands that talk, flowers with heavy hearts, what possibility would I dare deny?

Now she is Adrea. I am the mother who never conceived. She is the child that entered this world soundlessly, as silent and swift as a drowning. But I must not think of these things together.

I became Adrea's foster mom nine months after I met her. After I named her, I didn't see her again for a month, then I saw her every day for eight months, then she came to live with me.

From my office window at the Hearing Center I could look down over the backyard. The flower and vegetable garden had become a favorite place for many of the children. We started a class for foster children in June. Two mornings a week the foster kids from the Huntington School would come to the Deaf and Hearing Center for Families while our program was on trial. I met Adrea for the second time, after our day of self-introductions in her classroom, on the first day of the foster kids' class. I saw her name on the roster—Andrea Martinez. I decided I'd still call her Adrea.

On her first day I took her on a walk around the garden, showing her our plantings. She signed, "I know the names of everything in this garden." We circled around again. She pointed and signed, "Tomatoes, corn, leafy, carrots, vegetables, daisies, roses, yellow flowers, flowers." We circled around again. I pointed and fingerspelled the ones she hadn't known. "L-E-T-T-U-C-E," "Z-U-C-C-H-I-N-I," "S-Q-U-A-S-H," "M-A-R-I-G-O-L-D-S," "S-N-A-P-D-R-A-G-O-N-S." I showed her the crayon signs the other kids had made to label each thing. She was five and hadn't been shown the English alphabet yet.

The next day I took the subway from the Hearing Center down to the Huntington School. I found the old classroom. Approaching the teacher, I said, "I'd like to invite one of your students to attend the Deaf and Hearing Center every day after school." Adrea sat in the book corner watching me talk to the teacher. "I think she'd really benefit from it," I added. The teacher seemed to have an automatic no, "They're all foster children; the state won't pay the tuition."

"I'd like to offer a scholarship," I persisted.

"For which student?"

I said, "Andrea Martinez." She replied that I'd better call Mrs. Carter, her temporary foster mother. I phoned Mrs. Carter and told her about the Hearing Center. She said Adrea had better be home by 5:30. Dinner's at 6:00.

I went back into the classroom. Adrea was standing by the door. I approached the teacher, and signed, "Mrs. Carter said Adrea may come to the Hearing Center—" Adrea grabbed my hand. That afternoon I put Adrea's name on a cubby, a coat peg, and the chalkboard, and in a file in my desk.

Megan and Adrea would have had a few things in common. When we were children Megan drank tea. My mother would make her a whole pot of raspberry or peppermint tea, and she would draw at the kitchen table while drinking her tea. Now at work I always drink tea in my office before facing the students or staff. I like to be alone and listen to the radio before beginning a mostly silent day.

When Adrea first attended the Center, she would come upstairs to greet me. I fixed her tea with milk and honey. Then it turned into our alone time, during which Adrea and I got to know each other by starting our day together, sometimes we wouldn't sign at all. I would listen to music and Adrea would examine my things. Or we'd sit on the floor by the window and drink our tea and look out at the garden.

One day in those early months, I was upstairs in my office alone. It was free-play time, and I was supposed to be making some phone calls; instead I stared out the window. Adrea was alone in the herb garden. The head teacher, Maritza, had given her some basil sprouts to plant. I watched her pop the young shoots out of the plastic tray, gently, affectionately. Adrea has a green thumb, I was thinking. She stopped her work to examine her hands. She was looking at the black soil on her palms. I've seen deaf children sign their thoughts to themselves. I watched to see what Adrea might say. She rubbed her hands on her thighs, staining her jeans. She looked up. I was jolted out of my reverie—Adrea leaped up, stepping on the basil plants; she was running. Then I saw Sara, another child, in the yard. She had been riding a tricycle and was on the ground, her leg stuck in the tricycle, convulsing violently. Adrea kneeled on the ground by Sara's head. She looked around the yard frantically and, seeing no one, opened her mouth in what must have been a plaintive cry.

I was momentarily glued to the window. Before thinking anything else I wondered what Adrea sounded like. Then I bolted down the stairs. I removed the tricycle from underneath Sara and cradled her head in my lap. Adrea, Maritza, and the other children watched the end of Sara's seizure while crouching by her feet.

While the paramedics examined Sara, I held Adrea in my lap. She began crying in great heaving breaths. I rocked her in my arms. Kissing her damp forehead, I made small comforting sounds out of instinct, not logic. When she opened her eyes, I made the simple I LOVE YOU sign. Maritza placed her hand on my shoulder; I realized I was also crying.

That night was the first time I thought about adopting Adrea. Pacing in my apartment, I imagined her being there. How do you miss someone who has never been with you?

Adrea is like the little prince. She too does not let go of a question once it's asked.

I read, "He didn't realize that for kings, the world is extremely simplified: All men are subjects."

"What are subjects?" Adrea asked.

"They are people who follow the king." She signed the line over again; it struck her as extremely funny. How a king perceives his subjects—a historically depressing thought to me. I read the next two pages, signing through Adrea's uncontrollable laughter, her amusement building with each maniacal command put forth by the king. She rolled with her giggling, heedless of my disapproval. My opinion flagged. The king is every subject's fool. There is something to say about what amuses a child. Children are much better at recognizing the absurd. I asked Adrea if there are real kings. She pointed to Antoine de Saint-Exupéry's drawing. "No. They just wear clothes like this and sit on a chair like this. But the crown and the throne, they're real."

The easiest way to confuse me. Real or unreal.

Adrea's noises: she made a laughing noise and a crying noise. She would sometimes yell out in surprise or fear. There was a little fluff of voice that accompanied her sneezes and coughs. She made the Pa sound in signing, and the ponylike lip-blowing, both more exhalations than speech. She didn't utilize any speech. I first made an effort with her at the Hearing Center, before she was mine. Many of our children study speech. Adrea was resistant from the start, walking away to sit alone at an empty table.

Adrea was born deaf to a teenage mother. She was fifteen months old when her parents determined she was deaf. They left her at the hospital, and she became a ward of the state. I imagined that she remembered being a baby, parents that spoke into her face. When she was a baby she knew there was something, a sense she was not receiving.

In the weeks that I considered adopting Adrea, I would lie in my bedroom at night and try to calm myself. Fantasies of having her as my own were interrupted by negative thoughts. I imagined, if Adrea were down the street and I on the stoop or at the corner, not being able to call out her name, call her to me. The sound of my voice would never be known to her. I could never play music for her. Would I be able to handle her? Did I really know her? These thoughts burned in my head.

My inner voice of reason asked what motivated me to adopt a five-year-old deaf girl. I asked myself all the questions. I wanted to be a mother. I was a single woman, concerned with overpopulation; I did not want to bring another child into the world. It made sense that I should adopt a deaf child: it is hard for them to get placed, I am the director of a center for deaf children. I fell in love with Adrea. She was not replacing Megan. I was not still the eight-year-old left to my own devices. I met a child who was no one's, whom I wanted to be mine.

During the time that my foster care application was being processed and Adrea was still living with Mrs. Carter, I was always aware of my heart. It beat too fast, like a newborn's, and I walked around with my hand resting on my chest, hoping to quiet the worried organ.

One day I came down from my office, where I had been looking over the accumulating foster care papers. I needed to have a look at Adrea. All the time actually, I was stealing looks, trying to accustom myself to the idea of my daughter, us a family. I stuck my head into Maritza's reading group, looking around, and signed in concern, "Where's Adrea?" Returning my hand to my heart.

Maritza shook her head at me in reproach. Trying not to disrupt her class, she signed quickly with one hand, "She wanted a nap today."

Walking back to the resting area, I wondered if Adrea normally took naps. I saw her lying on a cot, her back to me, one small hand hanging over the edge. As I looked at Adrea's hand, she pulled it up toward her face, out of sight. She whined, and her hand fell back; it was smudged red. What's on her hand? I ran around to her other side. Her face was covered in blood; starting from her nose, the bottom of her face, her lips, her neck, her hair and ears, was blood. She was still asleep. I wiped her nose, and fresh blood appeared from her nostrils. I ran for Maritza.

"It's probably just a nosebleed." She closed the storybook firmly, unable to protect her class from my anxiety. Maritza asked the children to excuse the interruption; she reached for a towel by the sink.

I signed, "I'll get the first aid kit!" I was stopped short by Maritza stomping the floor for my attention. When I turned, her face was angry. My hand flew to my chest.

ANNA, she made my name sign sharply, her eyebrows pointed. "You do this," she held the clean towel out to me. "You don't need the first aid kit, it's a nosebleed, take care of her." She pulled my closed hand away from my chest and hung the towel on my arm.

With Adrea's head tilted back over my curved elbow, the weight of her in my arms, I applied gentle pressure against her small cublike face; her eyes looked placidly at me. I cleaned her face, all around her cheeks and mouth. I would get her hair and neck and ears when I was sure it was stanched. I was holding her, and her inside hand lay calm against my breast, and my heart beat steadily.

Pablo had been my first serious relationship; we were together all through college. After graduation we both dated other people but remained close friends. He spent most of his twenties split between New York and France, his childhood home. Pablo is a poet and teacher. We'd had an on-again, off-again relationship through the years, but we'd drifted apart since he began living with his girlfriend, Lindsay. I wanted to share with him that I'd met Adrea and was going to become a foster mother. We hadn't spoken in about six months, and I called him at home.

"Anna! What a nice surprise!"

I sensed that Lindsay was in the room with him. "Yes, it's been a while, how have you been?"

"Good. I'm teaching, winding down for the semester, work is good—I mean the writing, I'm just finishing another book."

"Pablo, that's wonderful, I can't wait to read it."

"What about you, what have you been up to?"

"I'm doing well. Work is good, the Center's gotten some new grants, we're expanding a bit. I've got some big news actually."

"What's going on?" Pablo said cautiously.

I pictured him standing in his apartment, the phone to his ear. I kept talking, "I'm going to be a foster mom. We started a foster care class at the Center, and there's a little girl I've grown very close to. She's in a home now and I'm applying to have her."

Pablo paused for a beat. I imagined that he was picturing Adrea in his mind. "Wow, Anna! That's huge. Have you thought it all through, I mean, of course you have."

"She's a very special girl."

"I'm sure. I just didn't know you would want to be a single mom."

I paused, feeling unfairly pigeonholed by someone who knew me too well for that, "I want to be her mom."

"Congratulations. I'm really happy for you. When can I meet her?"

"I'll call you once she's settled in and we'll make plans."

A month later, Pablo came by the Hearing Center to meet us after closing, and the three of us went to eat in a restaurant. When he arrived at the Center, Adrea and I were sitting at a child-height table drawing pictures. I felt a rush of warmth and nervousness because he was the first person outside Maritza and the staff to meet Adrea. I signed and spoke, "Pablo, this is Adrea. Adrea, this is an old friend of mine, Pablo."

Pablo said, "Oh! I didn't know," and then stiffly waved his hand back and forth, smiling broadly at Adrea. Adrea gave Pablo a brief look and went back to her drawing. We both sat at the table and watched Adrea. After a moment Pablo said, "I don't know why I didn't put it together that she was deaf."

"I guess I didn't say." I saw Adrea through Pablo's eyes. She was so separate from me, someone else's child, and in the moment seemed indifferent about both of us. I felt the weight of this new responsibility in a way I hadn't before. Pablo took up a sheet of paper, drew a smiley face, and pushed it toward Adrea. He waited expectantly for her to respond to the picture. When Adrea ignored his drawing, he took it back, added eyelashes and ears with earrings, and again slid it over to her. Adrea looked at it this time and signed to me HAIR, still avoiding any contact with Pablo. I told Pablo her suggestion, and he again took back his picture and drew long brown wavy hair, like Adrea's, around the face. I felt grateful for his effort.

During our Italian dinner, Adrea signed only to me, and I mostly translated what she was saying to Pablo. Pablo and I didn't manage to talk or catch up between us. Later that night after I'd put Adrea to sleep and gotten into bed, I felt lonely.

I tried a little bit in the following year to keep in touch with Pablo, but the reality of my being a new mother was consuming. My life was about getting to know Adrea, the daily routines of maintaining a household with a child.

During that year I would awake with the same recurring dream. In the dream I'm eight years old and I'm standing in the doorway of our childhood playroom. Directly across from the door, against the wall, Megan sits playing with a doll. I call out to Megan, overjoyed to see her, but she doesn't seem to hear me and continues playing. A wall of water pours down between us. Now Megan looks up, frightened; she reaches for me with her arms. At this point I realize I am dreaming but cannot pull out of the dream. Megan and I lock eyes. I call out, but she can't hear me. The water increases and we can no longer see each other. I would wake up breathless.

Sometimes I would quietly enter Adrea's bedroom while she slept, still needing to steal looks at her. I could come into her room at night clanging pans, singing anthems, shouting *Fire!* I used to worry, standing over her sleep, that a moonbeam would catch my belt buckle. A quick glimmer in the dark would startle awake a deaf girl.

I always asked about her dreams. At first, I was shy to ask. "Is there color? Are there animals? Are they silent, do people speak with their hands?" Her dreams were full of color, movement, and beautiful forms, almost always animals. Just like me as a girl.

One morning I entered Adrea's room early, while she was sleeping deeply. I took *The Little Prince* off her shelf and sat cross-legged on the floor to look at her. Her arms were flung above her head. Perspiration shone along her hairline. Her legs lay on top of the covers, feet together making a diamond shape. Her dark hair was begging its way out of her braid.

"I had a bad dream, Adrea." I spoke to her. "An hour to go before you wake." I rose, taking the book back to my bed. Adrea would come to me when she woke up.

"I have also a flower."
"We do not record flowers," the geographer said.
"Why not? It's the prettiest thing!"
"Because flowers are ephemeral."
"But what does ephemeral mean?"
"It means, 'which is threatened by imminent disappearance.'"
"Is my flower threatened by imminent disappearance?"
"Of course."
My flower is ephemeral, the little prince said to himself, and she has only four thorns with which to defend herself against the world!

Following the little prince, Adrea asked to plant her own flower surrounded by a ring of stones. She wanted to plant a single rose that would live forever. I said they only grow on a bush. Adrea protested that they sell one rose at the farmer's market; every Saturday we would go, on the way home buying a single rose.

Adrea lectures me, "My cut rose always dies and I can't plant one rose because they only grow on bushes. Now I don't have one special rose that I love and that loves me."

"We can grow lots of things in the garden, but when the winter comes, they will eventually die."

Adrea wants to know if dead things still love.

"I know living things can love dead things. I don't know about the other way around." Adrea says yes, dead things love living things a lot. Before Adrea, I had easier answers. Before Adrea, I had fewer answers, fewer questions. I had less.

An animal that lays eggs. A nesting species. To nurture something outside the body with fierce devotion. To wait separately for an arrival. To circle endlessly. This is an adoptive mother.

There are two kinds of deafness, volume and nuance. Being deaf actually means both. Hearing loss can be either. If only volume is involved you are not deaf. Volume can be solved with a hearing aid. For nuance there is nothing. If the ear cannot pick up tone or emphasis, nothing can be done.

I took Adrea to a specialist. Three hours, her back rigid on the table, instruments probing her. Piercing, whistling, dog sounds. Lack of response. I smiled at her throughout and told myself it didn't matter.

In the cab, on the way home, Adrea signed, "You wish I wasn't deaf."

"No! I just wanted to know. If you could use hearing aids, we would have gotten some, if they would help." She curled up on the seat, head in my lap, muffled sobbing of the deaf. The driver glanced in his rearview mirror.

A couple months after Adrea moved in, my parents flew out from Berkeley to meet her. I'd had many conversations with my father over the phone about her. He was support-ive and enthusiastic, wanting to know how he could help with money, education, things I'd need. I kept telling him, "Just be a grandpa."

I told Adrea that my mom and dad were coming, that they were very excited to meet her. She accepted the infor-mation without curiosity. I prepared my dad for Adrea's shyness; she'd only met Pablo so far and had largely ig-nored him. They came straight over from the airport. We would have dinner at my place and then they would go spend the night at their hotel.

We both greeted them at the front door. My father and mother wore giant smiles; they had practiced signing HELLO, NICE TO MEET YOU, and the exchanging of names. My mother pressed a teddy bear into Adrea's hands before even entering the apartment.

We settled in the living room after dinner. Adrea sat on the floor with a monkey stuffed animal she'd brought from Mrs. Carter's home. The bear from my mother sat in an armchair untouched. I asked Adrea, "Do you want to tell my parents about your school?" She shook her head no. I told her, "They have a nice garden at home, just like at the Hearing Center." Adrea lifted her monkey by the arms and shook him, ignoring my remark. "What's your monkey's name?" I signed to her and said aloud, but she wasn't look-ing to see what I'd said. I decided to talk with my parents and leave her be. We chatted about their work, the Hearing Center, Adrea's school. I kept glancing at Adrea, growing uncomfortable with her silence. Eventually we stopped talking and I watched Adrea playing on the floor, seemingly unaware of our presence.

I said, "I don't know why she's being this way."

My mother was staring at Adrea too. Her eyes never leaving the child, she said, "She's fine. She's just being a five-year-old."

My cheeks burned with shame; I needed Adrea to perform for them, but they didn't. The reality of Adrea, a five-year-old girl brought into our family, was an unspeakable shock. There was a harrowing truth, that we all three, even my mother, worked to get past. No one was relaxed during our short visit.

When my parents left to go back to their hotel the second night, we said goodbye. They would be going directly to the airport in the morning. Before leaving, my father asked me if I needed help, perhaps a part-time nanny to make things easier. I said, "No, no, we're still just settling in together. We're going to be fine." He stunned me then by saying, "It's wonderful what you're doing. We could have done the same."

The following day, alone again, Adrea and I went roller-skating in Central Park. We got caught in a summer storm and raced home. I made my rounds of the apartment, shutting the windows against the rain, the ledges already soaked. The windowsill in her room was a puddle. The blue curtain wet and heavy. I leaned out the window and twisted it in my hands, wringing out the rainwater.

From the kitchen, I could hear Adrea's skates badgering the floorboards. She could not hear my crying. If I lose this child. If God loses this child. I closed and locked the window. I remembered my parents from an earlier time, when they had just lost their youngest child.

I had been counseled by a social worker before considering adoption; she tried to prepare me for becoming an adoptive parent, telling me that it is integrally different, at first, from having a child. She said I would be asking myself questions that a biological parent would never entertain. That I would find myself wondering, "Why her? Was this the right child?" I did not tell her that I had met Adrea and then decided to adopt, instead of the other way around. I did not tell her that there were larger questions and doubts in my mind. One thing she said stuck with me. She warned that in the beginning an adopted child is not your child. You will love her before you will feel at ease with her. You will feel false, unwilling to find anything trying, tiring, or unpleasant about caring for her.

"You will watch yourself with her, from the outside." She guaranteed it would be a moment of frustration, an admission of anger, in which I would discover she was mine. She swore I'd recognize the moment. She was right. I'd been sleeping poorly for about a month while waiting for Adrea to move in, then we both had insomnia, and when she finally slept, I watched, wondering at having brought her so entirely into my life. I fretted over our mutual awkwardness, remembering the unchallenged ease of our previous relationship.

One Saturday morning I was finally sleeping; although it was probably only eight in the morning, I was luxuriating in sleeping in.

At first I thought it was my anxiety waking me, as from a nightmare, an abrupt shock. But once I was awake, there was a second crash, quieter and more glassy than the first. I ran into the kitchen. Adrea was standing on the counter by the sink. The hanging rack for pots dangled from one chain; the cast iron pans that had been released had rushed straight down into the cart of glassware. The broken glass and pans were all heaped up in a pile, as though they had already been swept. Had Adrea been afraid, the moment would have been delayed. Perhaps such an accident is not frightening without the sound effects. She jumped off the counter, avoiding the mess, and scooting her way out of the kitchen, signed, "You sleep later than Mrs. Carter."

I grabbed her arm as she headed past me, surprising us both. "What were you doing?"

"Nothing."

"I'm going to clean this up. Go into your room," I signed with pointed enunciation, my face compressed. "You are not allowed to play in the kitchen by yourself. This is a rule. Do you understand?"

Adrea ran down the hall to her room. As I stooped to pick up the larger pieces, it occurred to me that I was angry with her, in dire need of my own space, desperate for solitude, and finally, that these were the feelings of a tired mother toward her trying child, her child.

A year after we'd been together, we developed a routine of going to the antique flea market on Twenty-sixth Street; it served us better than any playground. Usually, in crowds, because she cannot hear me, Adrea stays by my side. Yet somehow at the flea market, she is a boomerang. Taking off there, touching back here. I walk up and down the rows. We keep a distant eye on each other. The mother of a deaf child grows to appreciate a controlled environment.

We are well known on Sundays. There are two antique dealers who sign, and who have become like uncles. Benson is the child of deaf parents and a great storyteller. Adrea will sit cross-legged in his stall and forget all about our shopping. Benson is in his sixties. He has lived in the city his whole life. He asks Adrea, "Do you know what happened in nineteen twenty-nine?" She thinks about it a long time. He turns away, gives the history of a particular rug to a potential buyer. I watch my daughter. She believes that she knows anything if she just has enough time to remember. I love that about her. "What would possess a deaf couple to have a child the year the stock market crashed?"

Adrea frowns in misunderstanding.

"That's the year I was born."

Adrea smiles happily. This makes perfect sense to her; she would probably have guessed this answer. I expect her to sign the year of her birth, but she is anxious for Benson to continue with the story. She doesn't bother with herself.

Martin is a young man with clunky hearing aids. He and Adrea spar, trading jokes, even gossip. He's only a couple years out of the Huntington School. She catches him up on the old-timers, teachers who never change from year to year. She's in first grade, he couldn't be older than twenty-one. Her ties with the flea market men are stronger than mine are. They are her friends.

We have bought our rugs from Benson. We each have dressers in our bedrooms from Martin. Almost all of our furniture is from the flea market, found items, or hand-made. Our square kitchen table, we painted blue-green, with flowers and turtles, stars and smiling teapots. I inscribed each side with a line from a children's song: All I Really Need—Is A Song In My Heart—Food In My Belly—And Love In My Family.

One day while we were visiting a plant nursery a gray-haired lady spoke to Adrea about the violets. "They're African violets. See those fuzzy leaves? You can't get those wet. So you have to be very careful when you water them. They like to be warm, but not right in the sun."

It took me a moment to realize this woman was talking to Adrea, who was fingering the African violet leaves. Did she know the lady was speaking to her? I came closer. Adrea's face was down close to the plant. Touching a hairy leaf to her cheek, she was smiling. She startled when I got in front of her, and signed to me, "Aren't these so sweet?"

I answered her, "This woman is telling you about them." I heard the surprised *ooh* of the flower lady. "They like warmth, but not direct sunlight. You can't get the leaves wet at all." Adrea responded immediately to the frailty of the plant, taking her hands off and then gently petting the pot. "Want to get some?" I asked. She nodded furiously. So this would be her flower, her fox, her little prince.

At home she looked up the plant in our botanical book. African violet. Nothing appealed more to Adrea than the perfection of that beautiful name for these warm, caterpillar-like plants. She drew a picture in her thick sketch pad. African violets with pink and purple flowers, jade green leaves with gray fuzz on them. The picture is propped against the window in the living room, the three plants lined up on the sill in front of it. Adrea uses my mother's old creamer with cracked blue and white enamel, fills it with water, and lifts the tender warm leaves, tipping water beneath them.

At the Hearing Center, the kids work in pairs or do individual writing projects at small tables. When the teacher wants their attention, she stomps her foot on the floor. Twelve heads turn up. To end playtime we flick the lights. Sometimes the hearing teachers smile at each other because of thunder cracking, or fire truck sirens, or cursing from the street that occurs unbeknownst to the children.

At the Bronx Zoo, they were drawn like magnets to the incessant roaring of the lion. Twelve deaf children, turning their heads looking for something, they did not know what. They were lured away from the soundless seals by the reverberation of a roar. The roar of a lion that is nowhere to be seen, a roar of such magnitude is to be felt.

Adrea tells me, "I know when a dog is barking at me. It sounds like this"; she throws her hands up in my face, flings all ten fingers before my eyes. She can put her hands on the big speakers at home and dance to the rhythm. In my office, she'll touch the radio to see if it's on. At home, we've connected lights that flash when our doorbell rings. On the telephones there are light bulbs that announce a call. I try to imagine when Adrea is older, her being home alone, seeing those lights blink.

Every night Adrea takes an hour-long bath, using almost an entire bar of glycerin soap. The green and yellow bars become wild fish, flipping out of her hands to escape. Loitering in the hall outside the bathroom, pretending to give her privacy, I manage to be afraid even of this innocence.

Saint-Exupéry met the little prince in the Sahara when his plane had to make an emergency landing. He needed to fix his engine before his water supply ran out. After a few days he awoke to a child's voice asking, "If you please, draw me a sheep."

Adrea loves riddles. "The stars are beautiful because of a flower that cannot be seen."

I've read her this line dozens of times, signed its incomprehensible phrasing to her over and over. Adrea also loves to sign this riddle. Her fingers flicking the stars, the wave over her face of BEAUTIFUL, her small hand growing a flower out of her other hand, and finally, the "cannot be seen." It has some unknown meaning for her. Yet another thing I can't understand about my own daughter.

I curled up in bed, my face to the window. I looked at my hands. They care for Adrea. They speak to Adrea. These hands have touched Megan. These same hands. Saint-Exupéry is tender toward the little prince because of his fragility and because he is loyal to a flower. I didn't want to feel that way about Adrea, loving her for her vulnerability or her loyalty. And in reality she is tough and durable. She is not returning to some small planet. We live together on the same island.

I felt Adrea climb up on the bed behind me, her silent warmth against my back. I turned over. Her face was flushed. I petted her forehead. "Hot puppy girl," I signed, "I think you have a fever."

She yawned in my face, staring at the book cover, her pupils dilated. She pressed against my shoulder, closing her eyes. I smoothed back her hair, imagining her time spent at the hospital while they found a foster placement for her at Mrs. Carter's. When I shifted in bed, she opened her eyes again heavily.

I got up and signed, "I'm going to squeeze some fresh orange juice."

She stood up on the bed, wanting to be held. Carrying her down the hall, I stopped in the bathroom, opened the medicine cabinet, and signed THERMOMETER. She took it off the glass shelf. I shifted her to my back and trotted down the hall to the kitchen. Bringing down a fever I could do.

~

My mother's brother, Ben, was waiting at our house when we came home from Cape Cod after Megan drowned. It was difficult to comprehend that Megan was dead, had died, partially because we had no body. Ben looked at us in shock. His wide-eyed expression made me think he was angry with me. I expected him to turn on me, saying, "Where were you? What were you doing?"

At times, I think terminal illness is better than accidental death. You have time while the disease worsens. But I suppose the dying would prefer an instant death. I suppose the dying would most prefer to slide underwater, gracefully disappear, causing so little trouble. Still, I envy the bereaved who can say, "It's a relief, an end to suffering, our good-byes were already said."

Those of us who were present were guilty. We stood by. No matter how much we fought to retrieve her, it was utter passivity. After all it was only water. She was in our hands a moment ago. No communal tragedy, no natural disaster. My parents, Carla, and I stood by. One child held on, one slipped away.

Ben was guiltless by disassociation. I think we needed his forgiveness. He had not been there; he had not failed.

His delayed reaction sent my mother into soundless sobbing, doubled over, her face a contortion of hysteria. He moved to her side, eyes still staring in disbelief. Embracing my mother, his gaze landed on me. He nudged my father toward the stairs. "Come on. All right now, all right. Let's go upstairs. You need rest." His voice was thick, "I'm sorry. I'm so sorry." He pulled me to his side. We climbed the stairs three abreast, my father right behind.

"You two lie down. I'm taking Anna to the store. We'll get food." He pulled down the blanket, leaned my mother back, pulled off her shoes, and tucked her in. My father sat on the other side of the bed. Ben kneeled on the floor beside my mother while she continued to cry. I stood behind my uncle. Now he was my buffer, and I wanted to be partnered with him one step outside this grief. And I wanted to leave the house.

I heard my mother whisper, "Everything hurts so much. It's like I have no skin."

Ben said, "This is the worst, Carolyn. This is the worst you'll ever go through. You're incredibly strong." I heard my name too. I knew he was telling her to be strong for me. He leaned over my mother and grabbed on to my father. "I'm here. I'll be here for anything."

Going with Ben was the best thing for me. I needed to tell the story. Not cry or be comforted, just to tell what happened. I told Ben from the beginning, everything, exactly. He had to pull off the road, hold on to the wheel.

"You know Carla has that yellow boat that we blow up?" Ben nodded, whether he knew or not. "Megan and Bonnie always sit inside it in the sand and pretend they're out sailing. And my mom and dad push them out in the water in it, to float around in the water. But it was my dad and Carla. My mom was on the beach with me, she was using the camera." I couldn't tell if Ben was listening. His face was down, one hand covering his eyes. I continued, "The waves were getting bigger. I think it was high tide. I wasn't swimming; I was standing with my mom." While talking I pulled on the loose threads of my jeans, scratched at my exposed knee. "A big wave crashed on the boat and we couldn't see anything for a minute. Megan fell out of the boat. I saw she wasn't in the boat, only Bonnie was, but I thought Megan was there, in the water." Ben's breathing was loud, catching in his throat. I knew I was upsetting him, but I had to finish telling it. "Nobody could find her. We were searching all around the boat. Mom went in the water. We all kept looking in the water." I felt I had to confess it to Ben. "I stayed on the beach; I didn't go in the water." Ben made no response. "I knew she was really lost. I knew we weren't going to find her."

Ben had no way of knowing that was the end of my story. It had no proper ending. I started crying. He said, "I just kept wishing you were wrong. You'd return home and it wouldn't be true." He took hold of my head, covering my ears with his large hands. He said, "I wish you could be spared."

Hadn't I been?

~

I needed to know that Adrea's placement with me would be permanent. The majority of foster care placements are temporary, providing children with safe environments while their parents work things out to get them back. But there are temporary placements that run on, turning into permanent adoption. It's very rare for a permanent adoption to dissolve, with the child returning to the birth parents. Yet this possibility plagued me.

Adrea's social worker assured me that Adrea fell into the category of permanent placement. She was not in touch with her birth parents, who had both been teens. They had left her at fifteen months old at St. Luke's Hospital. Child welfare had not been able to contact them in three years. She had no other next of kin. Under these circumstances it would be easy for me to apply for legal adoption, granting me the rights of a natural parent. Once she was mine, if her birth parents were to appear, there would be no question about my position. I would take whatever action to keep her.

The first six months that Adrea lived with me was under the label "foster placement." I received $370.00 a month from the state of New York for taking a disabled child into my home. We met with her social worker bi-monthly. After a year, I made a plea to the court to grant me guardianship, legal adoption. Her name was officially changed to Adrea Levy. Within just weeks we received an official-looking document from the court stating her new name and naming me as her legal parent. It looked surprisingly like a birth certificate. There was also an adjoining letter stating that I had relinquished all benefits of a foster parent.

I read Adrea's new "birth certificate" and pressed the paper to my lips in grateful appreciation. Adrea came out of her bath, dragging my big robe down the hall to me in the kitchen. She climbed up into my lap. I wrapped her up tight in the robe, rubbed her hair with the hood of it, and showed her what we'd received.

I interpreted the letter for her: "It means that you're my little girl now, that I'm going to be your mother, and we'll live together until you're all grown up." She was perched forward on my lap, hands flat on the kitchen table, twisted around to watch me. Then she examined the document again. When she finished, she leaned back against my chest, smiling. She pulled my arms around her, and raising my hands, made them clap together.

~

During my senior year at Columbia, Bonnie resurfaced for the first time since my childhood. I could only imagine her as a large-boned little girl with wavy sandy hair. I had seen her only a couple of times after Megan's death, and she never stopped representing the child that hadn't fallen out of the boat. I was not looking forward to the reunion. Strangely, Bonnie was starting college at Columbia, and my father asked me to look out for her. As usual my mother did not get involved.

Out of a sense of duty, I called Bonnie two months into the semester. I had put aside the evening, thinking she'd want to come see my apartment and that perhaps I'd cook her dinner. On the phone she said she was in the process of moving down to the East Village, she was enrolled in six classes, but she'd love to see me if I wanted to meet her at a jazz show at the Vanguard.

I told her I lived a block from the club. She took my address and said she'd come by first.

Looking at my bookshelves, the tapestry covering my bed, and the American Sign Language alphabet framed on the wall, she turned to me and said, "I pictured you differently."

"I didn't know what to picture either," I said. "We're pretty much strangers."

It was several months of seeing each other regularly before we discussed Megan. What a revelation. Bonnie was the third girl on the beach that day, the one in the water who didn't die, who mysteriously stayed afloat—as impossible as the one slipping under. She says she doesn't remember—not the drowning, not the beach, not Megan. She knows the story, of course; considers it an epic tale of her childhood.

Drinking tea in my living room, Bonnie told me, "I always knew when my mother was thinking about it, because of the way she looked at me, like I was lucky. It doesn't make sense for me to feel survivor's guilt, although I have."

"I think I'm also looking at you that way, as lucky," I said. "It's stupid, but then there wasn't much difference between the two of you."

"My mom never wanted to go to the beach house after that. We went a few summers, but she was so uncomfortable there, we stopped. And then my parents divorced." Bonnie wrapped both hands around her mug, peering inside. "I'm so sorry for you that she's gone."

Would Megan be like this forthright girl now? I didn't think so. I remember her at-times studied, careful movements, and her goofiness at other times. They were good friends though, Megan the thinker, Bonnie the doer.

~

My father came on a visit again after the adoption was finalized; this time he came alone. He watched Adrea closely as she cleaned up her blocks from the floor, as she brushed her teeth, as she signed to me. He had the palpable air of an observer. After we'd both tucked Adrea in bed and kissed her goodnight, I made us tea and we sat in my living room. My father told me a story.

When I was a newborn we lived in an apartment building in Somerville. The building mostly housed the elderly. It had a fenced-in little court in the front, with small plots of grass and benches. My mother was on maternity leave from Harvard, and she would take me down every day for air and sun. One night, when my father was coming home, a tiny old man called out to him, "Are you Anna's father?" My father told me that he recognized immediately that this was the first time he had been identified as my father. He shouted out, "Yes, I am!" How charming, he thought, that the first person to identify him as his infant daughter's father was an eighty-year-old man.

My father told me, "I was so excited with that, I thought about it for weeks. I always looked for that old man after that, especially when you were with me, so I could say hello and boast about my newborn daughter."

Moving restlessly around my living room, he described himself as a beaming new father, and then he turned on himself, flinging mud. He said, "I must have later taken fatherhood for granted. I must have. Because how could a parent lose his child, literally lose his child, had he not taken fathering for granted? He couldn't have." My father quit his pacing and sat forcibly in a chair. He continued, "We had already moved to Boston when Megan was born. That old man never saw or knew of Megan. But I thought of him after she died, and I was ashamed."

I wanted to just be sympathetic, but I felt incriminated for being the child he'd been vigilant with.

On his final night in New York, I got a sitter for Adrea, and my father and I went to see a Broadway musical. We walked at a brisk pace toward the theater, my father telling me an amusing story about his reading group in Berkeley. I laughed out loud; striding down Broadway, suddenly I could imagine him as a friend of mine. I marveled at the closeness I could feel in his presence, compared with the estrangement that seemed to construct itself with distance. I put my arm through his, he squeezed my hand.

We walked the next ten blocks in silence, and I imagined my father's thoughts had turned, like mine, to thinking about what had become of my mother.

My father would speak to Adrea, slowly, in a steady

voice. His signing is rudimentary. Adrea did a hilarious impersonation, fingerspelling H-E-L-L-O A-D-R-E-A H-O-W A-R-E Y-O-U?" Smiling broadly. Before he left he said, "She really is her own person, isn't she?" I was unsure if he had felt she was less of a person because she is deaf or because she was a substitution for another person.

Sign is like a voice or penmanship. It tells you something about a person. Adrea's signing is lazy. Her fingers are always slightly curled. She slurs. Deaf people sign much faster and less formally than hearing people do. We know a variety of families from the Hearing Center. Most commonly, families consist of a deaf child and hearing parents, like Adrea and me. I've worked with children who wish their parents were deaf. And I've heard of deaf parents hoping their unborn children will be deaf. It is not hard to understand. The desire for harmony.

Some families consist of two deaf parents and a hearing child. When I was a girl and I first thought about a hearing child of deaf adults, it seemed wrong to me, dangerous, a child in the wrong home. It was an outsider's view, a perspective that could only exist outside the Deaf community. Such a child would function as deaf with her parents and her Deaf community, and interact as any other hearing child in the hearing world. Then it was hard for me to accept. Now I know that what I objected to was my own place in my own home.

I think guiltily about Adrea. Over the years, I have worked with many hearing parents who sat before me and said, "We want to hear our child speak." I have tried to help, I work with them to communicate through sign and speech, but I have often felt a small judgment against those hearing parents who seemed to have a singular and unquestioned desire for their child to speak. As the mother now myself, I recognize this desire that seems almost biological.

I crave knowing the sound of her voice. If she giggles or cries, coughs or sneezes, I try to pick out the sounds that are her voice. Sometimes I almost hear the raspy tune of her. This yearning of mine doesn't justify wanting Adrea to attempt speech. Even when I tell myself that speech or reading lips will help her accomplish whatever she wants in the future, I still feel I'm betraying a proud Deaf identity.

About a year after I adopted Adrea, Pablo called. He and Lindsay had broken up. After that, we began talking on the phone at night after Adrea had gone to sleep. I looked forward to our nightly routine, and I welcomed having a grown-up to talk to, but mostly I realized how much I'd missed him.

Eventually we had a picnic in Central Park with Adrea. I cooked and packed a dinner, and Pablo brought red wine and a Wiffle ball and bat for Adrea. She shrugged when he handed her the bat and ball, and instead of taking it, she sat down on the blanket to eat. We had dinner and chocolate cake for dessert. Pablo and I drank the wine; we reclined on the picnic blanket, Adrea sitting cross-legged by our feet. She was watching us talk. She tapped my foot and signed, "Does he know sign?" I told her he didn't. When I told Pablo her question, he said, "I'm sure I know some signs!" He kneeled in front of her and emphatically said, "I do know a little," tapping his forehead and nodding his head up and down.

Adrea intuited his meaning and signed, "Show me, what?" Both her hands turned upward, pointer finger and thumb pinching the air, her lips pursed; it was obvious what she was asking him. Pablo laughed. He held his hand up to his face, thumb to nose, and waved his fingers, crossing his eyes. "How's that?"

Adrea shook her head, signing NO with both hands and laughing. "What else?"

Pablo patted the top of his head with one hand and

rubbed his belly with the other. Adrea looked at me, smiling, not sure if it might be something. I laughed. "He's fooling you, you'll have to teach him a real sign." Adrea thought for a minute and made a *P* in front of her nose, crossing her eyes. Pablo and I both laughed; "What's that?" I asked her.

"His name!" she said, pointing at Pablo. She'd given Pablo a name sign, a gesture I'd always considered a big honor.

Pablo stayed over at our place that night. It had been several years since the last time we'd made love. Touching each other, seeing each other naked, was sentimental and also bracingly new. Our lips and mouths learning each other's again, we undressed each other blindly, letting our hands feel the buttons and clasps. We paused between each garment to wordlessly acknowledge going further.

Having sex with Pablo cleared my mind of all present thoughts. I was only a body. My chest on top of his chest, thigh against thigh, my feet scratched his feet. His chest was hot; flashes of heat blew against my face. My body came undone. My hands fluttered around his head, his neck, flapped down his sides, his stomach. I moved through him, taking.

The next day he made us blueberry pancakes, which further established him as a friend of Adrea's. And before he went home that afternoon, he'd learned a dozen signs.

Pablo sent me an invitation to a reading promoting his new book of poetry. At the bottom of the flier he wrote, "There will be a sign interpreter, bring Adrea."

We got dressed up in a celebratory mood. I wore a long black skirt. Adrea wore a ballerina-style dress and a miniature leather bomber jacket we'd found at the flea market. She put on my vintage beaded headband, with her wavy hair hanging halfway down her back.

We both got dressed in my room. She stood in front of the full-length mirror, covering her mouth with her hands, apparently pleased with her appearance. It was rare for us to get dressed up.

Pablo's first poem was titled "Patois," about a family eating a native dinner of fish and garlic rice when a hurricane strikes. At the end of the poem you realize that there was no hurricane, it was only their conversation. I looked at Adrea watching the interpreter. She kept her face still, listening, though I'm sure she did not understand. His next poems were about a choreography of shoes in Grand Central Station, two children being pushed on swings by their elderly fathers, and a longer poem about an elegant woman, who I knew was his mother, ironing the clothes to bury her husband in. His last poem was dedicated to Adrea. I saw the interpreter smile at Adrea, who squirmed in her seat. The poem spoke of a girl who had magic hands that could pet hummingbirds, lift up the roof to see an airplane flying by, give the moon a sponge bath, carry sunlight into the middle of the night, tell stories, and keep secrets. The little girl had made a trade with an angel before she was born: all of these gifts in exchange for giving the angel her hearing.

After the reading, Adrea and Pablo had one of their typical conversations. She spoke to him in self-explanatory sign, something like mime or charades. He made up signs, most of them quite similar to the real gesture. After kissing him, she stroked her upper lip and dragged one hand down her chin, to comment on his new mustache and goatee. He responded by pretending to put on lipstick, the actual sign for "lipstick," which Adrea had insisted on putting on for the evening. He said, "You're the prettiest girl here," which I translated. She replied, "Thank you for the poem," which I told him.

He invited us to go have a drink with some friends. I said we were going home, pointing to Adrea, leaning heavily against my leg. We made plans for him to come over later when he was through. I told Adrea that Pablo would sleep over and be there when she woke up the next day. Yawning, she mimed to him that he would be flipping pancakes in the morning.

We took a cab home, and Adrea fell asleep leaning against my side. I rolled down the window to let the chilly air blow on my face. The car glided uptown without stopping; the night was perfectly clear. I saw people out walking their dogs, or arm in arm with their lovers, and I was happy.

The buzzer woke me at 12:30 A.M. I waited at the top of the stairs for Pablo to reach our floor. I was wearing a black slip. Pablo brightened when he saw me. "Sorry, I'm waking you." I just shook my head and smiled. He stretched his hands out and pressed his fingertips into my ribs.

"Come in." I backed away, laughing. I fed him cold chicken. There was a comfortable familiarity between us. I sat at the kitchen table, watching him help himself. I knew what I liked to look for in his face: his dark eyes, long lashes, shifting shadows. It was a few minutes before we started talking.

"You know, when I first saw you and Adrea signing, it amazed me that that was how you two communicated." He shook some hot sauce onto a piece of chicken, put the whole piece in his mouth. "The signing seemed like something for just the two of you, a secret language." He took another bite and continued, "She's such a beautiful little girl with her wild hair; she's alive like a lit wick, and so observant."

Pablo washed down his meal with a full glass of wine and poured another glass for sipping. I said, "She's all of that, true."

"I'm not making sense," he pointed at the wine accusingly, "all I'm saying is that Adrea is so special, she possesses some kind of magic."

"I'll accept that. Your poem was beautiful, she loved it."
I carried his dishes to the sink. "Let's go to bed."

As abruptly as we'd started we dropped the conversation.
He followed me down the hall.

I sat on my bed and watched him remove his shoes and
then his socks. He stood up and faced me, then leaned
down and kissed me lightly on the lips. "How've you been
Anna-bean?"

"I'm good, I guess I've been tired."

"What kind of tired?" He stroked my cheek.

"Tired like a mother." I gave him numerous small kisses
on the mouth.

"At-a-girl," he murmured.

This second time, we had sex as slowly as possible, making a game of it, stopping often and brushing each other's
skin with our fingertips. I felt myself memorizing the lines
of his body again. Afterward we lay resting for a while. I
saw his eyes were already closed. His sleeping face reminded me of the mornings I had awoken long before he
did and studied his slow-breathing mouth, smooth eyelids,
trusting neck. What amazed me back then, in college, was
that he didn't know about Megan. Until I told him, he had
no reason to pity me. I told him only when I knew he would
be meeting my parents.

I curled up next to him to sleep, but my eyes stayed
open, and I suddenly felt uneasy, as though something were
slipping away from me. I felt my heart accelerate. Pablo
sleeping in my bed again, the return of our relationship,
gave me insomnia. The world was happening, a turning
merry-go-round. His presence was an unexpected gift, but
wanting him to be there made me equally afraid.

Two days later, Pablo called me about his mother in
Paris. He was very worried. She was feeling lonely and in-
capable of handling daily necessities since her husband's

death. He told me, "She got lost in the city, driving his car, just got utterly lost and scared."

"I'm so sorry. It must be such a hard adjustment for her."

"She doesn't feel comfortable paying the rent and the bills through the mail, and yet she thinks the landlord is mocking her when they meet in person. She can't balance her checkbook. I never realized she was so dependent." His concerns piled up, not requiring any response from me.

Interrupting him, I said, "I'm sorry, but Adrea's in the bath and needs checking in on." In truth, I really didn't like hearing about people's mothers. I didn't like hearing people complain about what they do for their mother, or what their mother demands of them, or the inevitable heft of the relationship. I asked if he could come over for dinner and to talk later in the week. He said he might be going to Paris any day to help her; he'd call me back before bed.

Making my way down the hall to check on Adrea, I stopped outside the bathroom. The door was partially open, and I could see Adrea's reflection. She was standing in front of the mirror, her skin bright pink from the hot water. She was combing her hair back, moving her lips, pretending to talk. I reached my hand out to the wall to balance myself.

She did not look like somebody mouthing something without making noise. She did not know the shapes to make. Her mouth moved up and down like a ventriloquist's dummy. I turned away quickly, afraid for her to catch sight of me.

When I heard her feet squeaking their way back into the tub, I went to peek in on her. I pushed the door open and waved my hand until she looked up and saw me. She motioned for me to come in. I sat on the toilet and smiled at her. I said, "You've gotten so big. When did you grow?"

She smiled, pleased, "Every day." She turned around, tilting her head back, and handed me the cup to pour water over her. Kneeling down on the floor, I pushed my sleeves up to rinse her hair. I could remember my mother doing this for Megan and me. There were so many things Megan never did for herself. After I'd rinsed Adrea's hair, she sat up and turned to me, her eyes looking squarely into mine.

I signed, "When I was a little girl I used to sit in the bathtub and pretend I was a famous singer being interviewed. I would also practice sign in the bathtub until the water was freezing cold."

Adrea said, "You can go, I'm okay."

A woman came to see me at the Hearing Center with her infant son. We sat in my office and I closed the door, not yet knowing what she was there for. She told me her whole family was deaf, herself, her mother and father, brothers and sisters, even the cousins, aunts, uncles, deaf. When she was pregnant she knew the baby was deaf. But when the baby was born—she made the gesture for shock, her pointer fingers flicking out from under her eyes—he was hearing! It must be from his father's family. I know she will say it before she says it, and I am already nodding in understanding as she signs DISAPPOINTMENT.

After she left my office, I pictured Adrea in her classroom at the Huntington School. There were twenty kids in her class, all deaf, all signers. Sometimes when I picked her up in the afternoon to bring her back to the Center, I marveled at how she passed between worlds, from running around, signing back and forth with her deaf classmates, to the mixed sign and oral environment at the Center, to our home with a hearing mother. She seemed comfortable with each, but I wondered.

The day was threatening rain, but that never kept us from the flea market. First we went to see Benson in his usual stall. I worried that Martin would not have bothered with his heavy wood furniture on this gray day. Benson was delighted to have Adrea's company. We'd interrupted his breakfast of Cheerios eaten out of a tin camping dish. Although we'd already eaten, Adrea jumped at the offer of a bowl of what Benson was eating. He finished quickly, while she mouthed one little circle of cereal at a time. They were both getting ready for him to tell her a story of long ago. I put a sweater on Adrea, receiving one of her scowling looks, and asked Benson if I could leave her with him for a little while. Benson waved me away with an exaggerated gesture that won Adrea's utmost approval.

Martin was lurking around his own furniture as though he were loitering somewhere he didn't belong. His arms were folded over his thin chest; he was wearing only a light long-sleeved shirt. I had to resist the urge to find a sweater to put on him. Martin reminded me of a stray dog, speculative and wary, and clearly a loner. Still, he was the person I most wanted to talk to. I had gone to the flea market with an ulterior motive. I wanted to ask Martin about his schooling, his hearing ability, and most of all, his speech. He had gone to the Huntington School but must have had outside therapy for speech. He also wore hearing aids. Martin couldn't be a hundred percent deaf; only someone hard of hearing could have such highly developed speech.

He had a cigarette in one curled hand, which he dropped and stepped on the moment he saw me.

"Hi. I don't mind the smoke." He looked at me blankly, and I remembered that he's not the easiest person to talk to. "I was afraid you wouldn't be here today." I cut to the chase: "I want to talk to you about Adrea." As though on cue, I began speaking with my signing. Martin looked at me curiously, "About her learning to lip-read and possibly learning speech. I thought it would help to talk to you about your experience." I finally submitted to his silence.

He gave me an appraising look. "Is that what she wants?"

"She hasn't shown any interest in learning," I admitted.

"No? Well, most deaf children aren't interested; sign is their natural language," Martin said in his halting voice. I felt that he was making a point by using his imperfect speech rather than signing. His eyes were hooded as he continued. "I was resistant at first too. I was fitted for hearing aids at fourteen. I was taught to imitate sounds. I didn't think Adrea has any hearing?"

"That's right," I replied.

"It's a different process then. She must learn and memorize word sounds without knowing what they sound like." Martin rocked back and forth on his feet while talking; I felt as though he were deciding how much to share with me. "It's hard work, she'd have to really want to, and for what?"

I looked up as the first drops of rain hit my face. "I think it would make her life easier, when she's grown up."

"I suppose it does. She should decide." Martin started reaching for his tarps. Several people were examining his woodwork.

"Do you want help with that?" I asked.

"No, it's not much."

"I'd better get going. I'll come back around with Adrea to say hi."

Martin touched my arm. "I could picture Adrea going to Gallaudet University and doing anything she wants." He lifted a blue tarp lightly with his foot and smiled at me.

I smiled back. "Yeah, me too. I'll come back over. Want a coffee?"

He nodded yes and made the slang gesture SEE YOU LATER.

A few nights later Martin called me at home. The operator informed me it was a call from New York Relay. She would type my responses for a caller to read off a TTY. I wondered why the caller hadn't called directly to our TTY. Martin apologized for calling, adding that he thought he was in my neighborhood. He was at Columbia, attending a conference that he thought I'd be interested in, something about Adrea. I gave him directions to come over.

After I buzzed him in, Adrea opened the front door and waited for Martin to climb the three flights of stairs. She greeted him, "What are you doing here?"

I pulled her inside and asked him to please come in. Adrea took Martin to go see his furniture in our bedrooms. I put up coffee and took out an ashtray for Martin. When they returned to the kitchen, I gave Adrea juice and told Martin that coffee would be ready in five minutes. I put a pot of leftover soup on the stove while Adrea and Martin settled down at the table, talking. I always felt a desire to feed him.

Martin and Adrea repeated the same extensive handshake every time they saw each other, a ritual of the Huntington School. I carried two cups of coffee over to the table and placed the ashtray in front of Martin.

"I've been accepted to a six-week teaching program in Paris," Martin signed without preface. We always signed in Adrea's presence.

I couldn't understand why he had rushed over to tell me this. "Congratulations. What is it?"

"I'm doing a teacher training, for working with deaf children. They're enrolling children for speech therapy." Martin cocked his head toward Adrea, "Maybe you would like to apply."

I moved back to the stove to stir the soup. I wiped my hands on the front of my pants and walked back to the table. "Tell us more," I exhaled.

Adrea slapped her hand on the table, "What is it? I want to see."

"There's nothing to see. Martin is going on a trip to study in France. He came to tell us about it."

She turned her body full face toward Martin, excluding me from the conversation. "You want me to go with you?"

Martin looked at me before answering. "I think you might like to go too, with your mother."

I went back to the stove and turned off the flame under the soup; stomping on the floor, I asked Adrea to bring napkins and small plates to the table. I doled out three bowls of soup and cut slices from a round of bread. Carrying the food over, I said out loud to Martin, "Why are you going?"

He signed back, "I'm interested in teaching. I want to give up the furniture, make it a hobby."

His mouth lowered over the bowl; he worked his spoon in a continuous circular motion, devouring the soup. I swallowed mouthfuls without tasting it. I signed again, "What's special about it that you couldn't do here?"

Taking a rest, he signed, "It's very special, a first—"

Adrea jumped in, "Is it like the Hearing Center? Do they have animals?" Adrea strongly believed that the Hearing Center was lacking in the way of animals.

Martin laughed. "They have computers that we don't have yet in America." He turned to look at me. "Computers for developing speech for the deaf, very advanced."

I looked at Adrea, wiped the bread crumbs from the side of her mouth with my hand; she shrugged away. I knew she was mulling over the idea for herself. I knew she hadn't forgotten my earlier interest. She looked at Martin. "We don't have computers," she declared, then immediately turned her attention to her soup.

I questioned Martin about the program, how to apply, the process, what it cost. I was careful to behave casually. Adrea stood up and carried her and Martin's empty bowls to the sink. I waved her down and signed, "Maybe Martin would like some more." Her eyes bulged in embarrassment, and he quickly motioned that he'd had enough. Adrea left the room and came back with her crayons and pad, lying on the floor in the living room to draw, where she could still see us. I knew she was interested and nervous about our discussion, but yet she didn't want to be involved. She would take in this new development in increments, as she could handle it.

With her out of the room, Martin switched to speaking. "I think Adrea would be accepted." He removed his cigarettes from his pocket, asking with his expression if it was okay.

I nodded, pushing the ashtray toward him. "Why?"

"One, she's a foster child, and two, she's very young—"

"She's adopted and she's seven, older than she looks. Is that young for the program? Isn't it for children?"

"Yes," he exhaled out of the side of his mouth, trying to keep the smoke away from me. "For children and adults, students and teachers; I think she'd be accepted, Anna." It was the first time he'd spoken my given name aloud. I noticed how strangely the short syllables hung in his mouth. "Tell them about your center, and how you adopted Adrea. I think they'll accept her."

He picked up his pack of cigarettes, preparing to go. "Thanks, Martin—for coming to talk to us. And congratulations, you'll be a wonderful teacher." He blushed and ducked his head, not responding.

Before leaving, Martin went into the living room and produced from his jacket pocket a little toy for Adrea. It was a wooden donkey, four hooves planted on a little round stand. The donkey's body was made up of many small, hollow pieces of wood, with elastic strings running through it. Martin demonstrated that when you push the bottom of the pedestal, the toy does a jig. You can push different parts of it to make the donkey nod his head, or bend his knees, or collapse completely. Megan and I had played with the same kind of toy as children.

That night Adrea and I lay in my bed, going over the pamphlets Martin had left. We talked about speech. I said, "You know, sign is a language, just like English or Spanish."

"Sure. But if I could lip-read, I would know what everyone was saying, like Martin. Already I know when you say my name, I can lip-read 'Adrea.'"

I looked at her small face as I sat up on my bed in the dim light, knowing so much about herself already. "Do you remember when we talked about speech before?"

She raised her little shoulders. "I can't speak." Both her little hands vibrated somewhat wildly—the sign for talking through speech. "But when I grow up and live alone, I should know how to lip-read."

I shrugged, giving her a halfhearted smile. I lay my head back on the pillow. Her words "live alone" hung there, a warning—this child would one day leave me; my throat ached with that future loneliness. Adrea pressed against my shoulder, throwing one arm across my chest. We lay still a long time.

Later we ate popcorn in bed and read bedtime stories. Adrea jumped up to fetch the drawings she'd made while Martin was here. There was a forest with trees and a stream, and a little rabbit sitting up. The final picture she'd made was of herself holding a bunch of balloons.

I had met Maritza when we were both in our midtwenties, at a Deaf social event in New York. I was the only hearing person there. I watched her talking to three men, and I imagined their attraction to her. Later that night, I walked past her toward the kitchen for another drink, and she tapped my arm, "Are you deaf?"

"No, I'm a teacher, I work with deaf children."

"I'm also a teacher. What's your name?" We talked about our work, Gallaudet—where she'd gone to college—

teaching, and eventually our families. Halfway through our conversation she said, "Is your family bilingual, did you grow up signing?" I told her I started signing at age eight, because I thought I could speak to my dead sister. She just nodded her head, accepting.

Maritza later encouraged me through my decision to adopt Adrea, and she spoke to Adrea about it too.

One night at my house, examining the illustrations and lyrics I'd painted on the borders of my kitchen table, Maritza questioned me, "A Song In My Heart?" I told her it was from a children's song I knew from my early teaching years.

She signed, "Does Adrea know what it means to have a song in her heart? I don't."

I was stunned. Had I excluded Adrea by painting those words on our table? I felt like a failure as her mother. I was struck anew with insecurity. "Do you think I should paint over them?"

"It doesn't matter." Maritza studied me. "You are a good mother. You're just not deaf. You're hearing." She rolled her index finger in front of her chin for a long time, emphasizing the ability to hear. "You can't expect to know what it's like to be deaf, even through Adrea."

Sitting in my kitchen, my hands flat on that table without explanations for anything, my limitations laid out like cards, a trusted friend bearing witness, I thought I must learn to tolerate these shortcomings.

I was not a natural citizen of the community I most considered my own. Adrea and I had a separation that would always be there.

Laurent Clerc was a deaf teacher who migrated to Massachusetts from France. Thomas Hopkins Gallaudet was a hearing priest who lived in a Deaf community in

Martha's Vineyard. The two of them developed the basis for American Sign Language and started the first school for deaf children in America. The year was 1817.

Starting in the late 1800s there have been various movements against sign language in Deaf education. Misguided educators discouraged deaf students from using sign, thinking that the best way for them to assimilate was through lip-reading and speech. Signing was prohibited in Deaf schools. They would restrain children's hands so they could not sign. While signing was banned, deaf teachers and students secretly passed on the language. I have heard of Deaf communities in Canada that have used two sign languages, one to communicate with the outside world and a second sign language that no hearing person knows.

I came aboveground from the subway at 103rd Street and started walking home, remembering being eight years old and first learning about the history and importance of ASL. Sign was my salvation as a child. It was what I studied in college. Later, it was how I made my living and what led me into being a mother. Adrea and I would go to Columbia and interview for the French program next week as we'd arranged. But I was not going to persuade Adrea either way. As when I was a child taking ASL classes, I started signing my thoughts to myself, stepping down the street until I arrived at our doorstep.

Our appointment was at ten o'clock. I toasted English muffins and made chamomile tea to calm my nerves. We'd gotten ready too early and had an hour to spare before walking up to Columbia. Adrea was usually unbelievably slow in getting ready. She would brush her hair for more than twenty minutes, brush her teeth for five, and the time between putting on her underwear and her shirt could seem like hours. On this day, she came out to the kitchen quickly, fully dressed, even in shoes. She signed, "Are my sneakers okay?"

She was wearing a denim dress and Converse high-tops. "Yes."

We sat at the table, eating in silence. I mentally reprimanded myself for being so tense. We were going to find out if we were interested in this program. Perhaps she wouldn't even be accepted. Perhaps we'd decide not to go. My nervousness had steadily mounted since the week before, when I'd told Maritza about the program and that we might be away from the Center for six weeks if we decided to go. Maritza had only nodded. I went into the bathroom to brush my teeth again. I looked hard at my face in the mirror.

At times like these, when I felt that I didn't have any control, I would lose myself. The sight of my own eyes could ruin me. Right after Megan's death, I learned to handle things alone. I would stiffen my shoulders and hold a straight face and then make my own lunch, or shower or dress, or walk to the bus. But when I looked in a mirror, at my eyes, I saw right inside, and was caught. I would watch my face cry at itself.

Looking now, I could see that same faltering, like something healed but afraid to tear again. "Stop," I said to my reflection, and then forced a smile. I washed the makeup off my face and rubbed it dry with a towel.

"After the interview do you want to go to the zoo or the natural history museum?" I asked Adrea.

She nodded her head emphatically.

"Which one?"

"Both," she signed, raising her eyebrows up high.

We were led directly into a large office. There was a distinguished-looking Frenchman named Xavier and a young American man; they stood and greeted us by name. Adrea and I sat on a small couch together. Adrea ignored the two men and looked around the room. I settled in my seat and tried to be natural. The American led the discussion. He started by talking about what a personable young man Martin was; I stopped myself from looking surprised. We communicated in American Sign Language. I wondered if Xavier was fluent in ASL or if he was just vaguely following along. The American told us about the program in detail; gradually Adrea focused on his signing.

In the six weeks, the children would get acquainted with the speech computers, practice word sounds and mouth shapes, and develop speech-compatible breathing, and those with some hearing capacity would use high-intensity earphones to learn and memorize word sounds. These activities would take place among other traditional teaching methods.

I'd heard that French educators were strict disciplinarians. I was debating whether to ask about this when the interview switched to a questioning phase. They were social questions, meant to put people at ease; they inquired about my work and our interests as a family.

I told them I was a single mother, even though it was clear on the application. I told them about the Deaf and Hearing Center and my teaching experience. And since she had no prior experience with speech, I told them about Adrea's progress with reading and writing in English.

Xavier signed in ASL, for the first time since we'd arrived, "When I was a boy I went to a school and boarding-house for deaf children in France. I was the only child who had a mother. My mother came every holiday and brought me candy and money. The other children were orphans. This was very common sixty years ago." He nodded his head up and down and folded his hands in his lap. I felt at a loss for what to say. I knew he was referring to our application and Adrea's medical records, which indicated Adrea had been an orphan. He turned to Adrea. "Would you like to come to France?"

Her head dipped slightly. "Are you French?" she asked.

"Yes, I am French," he said with pleasure.

"Do you know the little prince?"

Xavier began to shake his head, his lips pursed out negatively, then he burst into laughter. "No, my dear, we have never met." And then kindly but firmly, "Would you still like to come to France to learn?"

MAYBE; Adrea moved her upturned palms up and down in the scales gesture. She shifted her eyes away, toward the window, leaned into my shoulder. She was ready to leave.

We spoke a little longer about the acceptance process, the competitiveness of the program, and what we would need to do in order to prepare for the trip. The American gave me a video to acquaint myself with Langue des Signes Française. He whispered as we left, "I intend to invite Miss Adrea."

I felt an immediate lift leaving the old Columbia building and stepping outdoors. My mood was completely altered from before the interview. I felt hopeful that we would go to France and that Adrea would enjoy it.

Adrea rushed at and scattered a small flock of pigeons half a block ahead of me. Paris would be exciting, I thought for the first time. Traveling would be expanding for Adrea. Because she's so observant, she's like an older child; I knew she would take away many impressions and memories. We would have a journey together. It had turned into a beautiful day. Taking off my jacket, I ran to catch up with Adrea.

The first thing people ask in a Deaf conversation is "Are you deaf?" It is the most important thing one needs to know. It is also exemplary of a cultural trait of directness. Deaf people are direct. Of course sign language can accommodate lies, but I am certain that the deaf lie less than hearing people.

The clear function of every signed phrase pleased me. "Are you deaf?" "The black girl," "the fat boy," "the one with the big nose"; always the most distinctive physical characteristic was used. It was not offensive; easy identification, clarity, was all-important. Even the sign for "dead" was without ceremony: two hands rolling over like a dog.

I started sign language classes shortly after Megan's death; its directness was a great relief to me. Sign filled a gaping void and took me away from the world of bereavement. Words of sympathy had exhausted my tolerance for words themselves.

I discovered there were different silences. My parents' new way of treating me, absent caresses, despondent non-responses, all imposed an unbearable silence on me. And Megan's evaporation was another silence. I found comfort by wrapping myself in the natural silence of the deaf.

Bonnie visited us from Massachusetts for the weekend. I'd never had a wide circle of friends, but without effort I maintained a close friendship with the one person who was Megan's friend. Bonnie had wholeheartedly supported my adopting Adrea. This trip to France was no different.

The three of us ate brunch in a restaurant off Central Park. Afterward we walked through the park. Bonnie kept picking up Adrea and spinning her in circles, or tickling her under her arms, to her delight. We stopped in the park outside the Metropolitan Museum, where Adrea started playing with an unleashed dog.

"She's crazy about animals, gardening too." The dog's owner handed Adrea a ball to throw for the waiting dog. "Sometimes I dream about moving out of the city," I said.

"Move to Northampton." Bonnie smiled. "I'm going to need friends around when I have the baby."

"What? You're pregnant!" I shouted in surprise. I stared at her and grabbed her around the waist in a hug. "I didn't know you were planning to have a baby."

Her face was bright and looked faintly mischievous. "Not

planning, just being careless, a happy accident." I hugged her again. Bonnie a mother. I felt so many emotions, about the life hardly begun, about the life long ago ended.

Adrea came trotting over, panting from keeping up with the dog. I told her that Bonnie was going to have a baby. She looked at Bonnie's flat stomach and said, "She's adopting a baby?"

"No, you smart girl," I said, "in her belly, it's just not big enough to show yet."

"Will you be a 'big sister' to the baby when it comes?" Bonnie asked.

I signed the question to Adrea. She nodded her head up and down, patting Bonnie on the stomach.

That night Bonnie and I sat on the couch in the living room after Adrea went to bed. I talked about the program in Paris and told her that I was waiting for an answer. She remembered my earlier hesitations and observed that they seemed to be gone. I admitted that I'd come around to really wanting it, but didn't want to push. "We'll see. If she's accepted, we'll have to talk about it. I don't think she's thought about the interview since we left. Going to the zoo was more significant," I conjectured, plucking lint from the throw blanket on the couch.

"Isn't Pablo in Paris?"

"Yes, but I wouldn't expect anything of him. He's there to take care of his mother. She's in a crisis since his father died."

I thought for the first time about Simon, Bonnie's long-term boyfriend. "How's Simon feel about the baby?"

"I was wondering when you'd get around to asking that. Well, when I told him, he decided right away that he wanted us to keep the baby. I needed to take some time away from him for the first few weeks because I needed to make my own decision. Now we're both feeling pretty sure about parenting together." Bonnie traced her fingertips over her stomach. "We're not as sure about marriage. I mean, we've been together nine years, it's not like we don't know each other well enough. But I think we both always thought it wasn't for life—as if the time so far hasn't been life." She paused for breath. I knew better than to try to interject. "We're both noncommittal. But who could I love more than Simon?"

I nodded. "Nobody," thinking about Pablo and me.

Bonnie shivered. "Why isn't there heat?" She pushed down into the cushions, sticking her feet underneath me.

I went for the feather comforter in my room but, changing my mind, called back, "Let's get into bed."

Bonnie came running down the hall. "I'm freezing," she said, rushing under the covers. "This was my throwing-up time of day, but I think I'm past that."

I looked down at her, huddled in the bed, her dark blond hair sticking out the top. I saw her five years old on the beach running with Megan. I hope she has a girl, I thought, with her cheekbones and pointed chin, her wide full mouth and stormy eyes. I got into bed with her. "Bonnie," I whispered, "what does it feel like? Being pregnant."

"Oh," she stretched out long on her back, already drifting toward sleep, "a lot of hormonal changes; I feel irritable but also more sentimental. Poor Simon." She turned toward me, "I'm so tired."

Bonnie fell asleep. My mind went to the afternoon two weeks earlier when Pablo called, saying, "Run down here and say good-bye to me."

"You're here? Your flight's in two hours!"

"So run, I'm in my cab downstairs, come see your man off." I told Adrea I'd be right back and I rushed down to the street. Pablo stood in front of our building, his cab idling behind him.

"You're crazy. You drove by here on your way to the airport?"

"The driver insisted," he teased. "I wanted to kiss you good-bye, I'm not sure how long this trip will be." He held out his keys. "I wanted to give you these too; would you hold on to them for me?"

"Sure." I took them nervously.

"You know what I say about 'sure.'"

"What?" I was smiling, already caught.

"It's an uncertain yes. I opened a P.O. box—you don't need to go by there, just hold the keys in case something happens."

I put the keys in my back pocket. "We may be coming to Paris in a month, if Adrea gets accepted into this program."

"I'm hoping you will. Give me a hug, I have to go."

The American program director we'd met called the following week. He was pleased to tell me that Adrea was invited to the spring session in Paris. I forced myself to focus on what I was being told. When his welcoming speech wound down, he said, "Do you want to go?"

"Yes." I was about to respond that my daughter had reservations, but I stopped myself. He wasn't the one I needed to work this out with. "Please give us a couple of days to talk about it and I'll let you know."

I picked Adrea up from school and brought her back to the Center. Instead of her slipping into the art class, I told her to come up to my office with me. Adrea ran up the stairs with my keys and opened my office. I followed her in and shut the door, put down our bags, and sat on a cushion on the floor in front of the window. Adrea plopped down beside me.

"Remember when we used to have tea right here every day?"

"Yeah, where's your mug?"

I pointed to the ceramic mug on my desk. Adrea asked, "Should we have tea?"

"Maybe in a little bit. I want to talk about the people we met last week with the school in France."

"Where Martin is going," Adrea stated promptly.

"That's right. They called to say that we're invited. We could go for six weeks and you would take classes there, just like being in school."

Adrea looked at my face and then drew one hand up and touched my lips. I pretended to bite her fingers. She smiled and looked out the window, now resting both hands on the low sill.

"I want to go if we'll be together," she signed, turning to me. "Do you want to go to France?"

I pulled her onto my lap, nodding yes.

Bonnie bought Adrea a beret, which Adrea began to wear every day. We studied the video on French signing. A young woman with a white button-up shirt stood full figure on the screen. She spoke and signed basic greetings and common phrases, first in ASL, then in French sign. I watched amused as Adrea practiced "May I have the check please" and "Can you help me find my hotel?" I called Pablo; he said he looked forward to showing us Paris. If his mother went out to the countryside as she kept swearing to do, then we could stay in her apartment. We would be boarding at the school though, so it wasn't necessary. I told Pablo what Adrea had said about the little prince at the interview. He laughed appreciatively. I could tell he was in need of some lighter company. We would do each other some good on this trip, I thought.

We socialized with Martin and Benson for the first time. We went on a picnic in the park the weekend after we learned Adrea was accepted. Martin was much more outwardly excited than I was. It was still largely surreal to me. With all of Benson's questions and sentimental contemplation, I began to feel sorry that he wasn't coming to France too. Benson took Adrea to run around in the grass while Martin and I discussed the trip.

I was surprised to hear that Martin was afraid of not

being able to use foreign currency. He claimed he could not understand money with a different value. He wanted to get traveler's checks and asked if I would help him. Martin is an arithmetic dyslexic. He said it's worse than being deaf, which I would love to believe.

I watched Adrea twirl around, her beret tilted on her curly head, clutching Benson's large hand. I wondered about what we were getting ourselves into.

We were washing dishes after dinner. Even though Adrea didn't need it anymore, she still liked standing on her wooden step by the sink. She took the clean wet dishes from my hands and wiped them dry. With our hands busy, there was no talking. I had music on and I was singing along.

I spent extra time scrubbing a pot, enjoying the song. Adrea stood watching me, her hands empty. She leaned over the sink in front of me to sign, "What is this song saying?"

I'd translated a lot of the music I listened to for Adrea, and she could recognize different types of music from the vibrations of the speakers. I put the pot down and wiped my hands. "It's a very wise song about how to be a good person. It says, 'It takes a whole lot of human feeling to be a human being.'"

"That sounds like a kid song." She touched my arm before I could start soaping the glasses. "Your little sister died, right?"

I jumped at the question. "Yes, that's right." She already knew this. "That picture on the piano is Megan. You know she was my sister, and she died."

Adrea looked strangely excited. She signed quickly, "Did she grow up?"

"No, she was still a baby when she died—well, not a baby, a little girl. She died a very long time ago."

Adrea leaped off the step and ran into the living room,

running back in with the picture in her hand. I didn't want to look at it. She climbed back up and held it out in front of herself, studying it. She wiped the frame with her dishtowel and placed it on the counter. "She was so cute. Was she deaf?"

"No. No, sweetie. She was hearing."

"Why did she get sick at the beach?" Adrea persisted.

"She wasn't sick, she drowned." There isn't a sign for "drowning"; you make the sign for "water" and then one finger swiveling downward, like a person sinking, and then the sign for "dead." My hands felt wrong.

Adrea picked up the frame again, trying to see the story I was telling her.

"Sweetie, would you go put that back on the piano?"

She ran from the room again. When she returned, she said, "Do you have more pictures?" "I do," I said, turning off the faucet.

"Can I see them please!" she hopped on her footstool. I dried my hands slowly. "Let's see if we can find them," I signed. We went into my bedroom and I pulled my childhood photo albums down from the closet shelf. We sat on my bed and I flipped the cover of one album, while Adrea craned over my lap to see. I turned the pages steadily, but Adrea examined the photos at a painstakingly slow pace, placing her hand on the pages to stop me. It was the same sort of enjoyment she took with her storybooks, innocent and curious. She pointed to almost every picture, saying she liked Megan's dress or shirt, or what a cute smile Megan had. I flipped the pages. I had not looked at them in a long time, and I had not thought of sharing them with Adrea, yet somehow I was still pleased for Megan to receive these compliments. I agreed with Adrea that Megan was very cute, telling her that she was smart and sweet too.

When she was finished I said, "Let's look at the other albums, of us, too."

"Okay. I think Megan was deaf. Was she?"

"No, she wasn't. Why do you think that?"

Adrea responded immediately, "Because you signed with her."

I weighed my words. "No, I didn't."

I kept my eyes trained on the picture centered on the open page. It is hard to sign to someone without making eye contact, but I couldn't meet Adrea's eyes. The picture before us was of Megan and me sitting side by side. I had my arm around her shoulders, and her hand leaned in my lap. We were both smiling at the camera; I was missing a tooth.

"When Megan died I was . . . I missed her, I was confused." The sign for this is like clawing at the side of your head. "I tried to talk to her. But she wasn't deaf and we didn't sign. I learned sign later by myself. Do you understand?" I finally looked at Adrea's face.

She nodded and made a single sign, SAD.

BOOK TWO

The morning Megan drowned we had hunted for seagull feathers. We most desired the ones that were clean and dry, the quills lying in smooth striations. The best ones had both white and gray on them.

Megan had collected a fistful; she ran from spot to spot, plucking them out of the sand to add to her bouquet. I worked more slowly, combing the beach in a zigzag. Each feather I found went through an inspection. After a few good finds, I would discard an earlier keeper, now too imperfect. My collection always outdid Megan's; she was too indiscriminate. She came bounding toward me, her voice lifting in the salty air, "Anna, how many do you have?" I looked up to see her smiling head bobbing in front of me, hair held up in the wind in babyish tufts, sand perfectly pebbled to her arms and chest.

"I have eight."

"You are eight!" she squealed. I disapproved of how easily she was amused. She was busy counting her clump of feathers: "I have sixteen!" She actually had fifteen; I saw her miscount. She handed me half of hers. "Are we even?" she asked, pointing at each one of our feathers, counting again. "Come on Anna, let's find more," she shouted, running off.

I bent over where I was standing, began picking through a pile of seaweed for feathers or shells. She raced up and down the strip of beach. She would have a hundred feathers by breakfast. She was my little sister. She died later that morning.

She slipped underneath, grasped for the sharp rocks shining; she remembered the last time her lungs had been filled with fluid, the same calm silence of the womb. She swam hard for the surface. She saw herself, a baby mermaid, hair streaming back, a last big oxygen bubble escaping her mouth. There were monsoon rains with every turn of her neck. Earthquakes broke fault lines with each kick of her legs. Every thrashing of her arms brought forest fires somewhere. Opening her mouth caused volcanoes to erupt.

In this way, she left us.

The twin bed, later to be Megan's own bed, was bought in the eighth month. There was a tiny nursery, a half room, where the bed was put. When my mother's contractions began, she put fresh sheets on the bed. My father fussed with bringing in an empty water basin, towels, flowers, and the record player from downstairs. And then later Uncle Ben and the three of us, and Sue, the "middle wife," which I thought meant she had an older sister and a younger sister, were there in the room.

Earlier there had also been Carla and Mannie. Carla had their new baby, Bonnie, strapped to her chest. I wanted to see her baby, and they all laughed and said that I wasn't sure what a baby was, and who knew what I was expecting. Carla said, "Anna could come to our house during the birth." I thought we were going to have a birthday party for our new baby. I said, "I always go to births, and this is my own sister's." I was sure it was a sister. My mother forgot to say "or brother" because everyone was laughing. I waited alone in the living room for the birthday to start.

They played cards and drank tea in the kitchen. Occasionally my mother breathed out hard and said *eew*, or held her stomach, running to the bathroom. I came into the kitchen and tried to sit on her lap. She said, "Anna, I can't right now," and pushed me away from her knees. Her face was sweating, and she went and stood by the sink. She ran the water and splashed her face. She glanced at me, and I walked over on my heels, my toes lifted up and my arms held out. "Funny girl," she said, "now we're going to have the birth." Carla and Mannie kissed her and left.

Upstairs, she lay on the bed propped on one arm, with one knee bent up. Sue said, "You still have such skinny legs, you're all belly." My father sat on the floor by the bed and put on a record, the Beatles, and held my mother's hand. I sat in his lap, and the talking went on.

My mother seemed fine again, like she'd been all month, big and comfortable, with the baby very big inside her, just resting on the couch or reading. I wanted to ask her when we would have the birth, but I didn't want to be laughed at. Then my mother started talking to me. Sue lifted my mother's nightgown up around her waist, and my mother said, "Anna, my body is opening, my vagina will stretch to let the baby come out." I looked at her exposed vagina, and I remember thinking it looked bigger than my whole hand. I said, "The baby will fit." She smiled and said yes.

My father said that I was born in a hospital and this was much better, to be at home. My mother talked only to me. She told me the baby was getting ready to come out. That the baby decided herself (sometimes she called her a girl too) when to come out of the womb, and now she was almost ready. When she came out, she would breathe with her lungs for the first time; she would cry getting used to the world.

My uncle Ben had gone to the store for something. Now he sat in a chair against the wall. He and my mother made jokes I didn't understand, about their mother and when they were children. My father sat at the foot of the bed, rubbing my mother's calves; he laughed at their jokes too. The midwife said she wanted to check my mom again; Ben went to wait downstairs for the baby to be born.

I sat on my father's lap. My mother started grunting and not talking to me at all; my father stroked her leg until she said all hands off her, she couldn't be touched. Sue said my mom was ready, open, and she could push. Sue kept telling her to push. I watched my mother's hands, expecting to see her pushing. I said, "Mommy, push." She laughed a sharp burst, but she didn't answer. I remember she raised up her knees, and I saw a white ball appear from inside her, and then the blood splashed on her thighs. I started screaming, and Uncle Ben came back into the room and carried me away.

I dressed Megan in black and white. We were doing a music recital for Mom and Dad, Carla and her husband, Mannie, and Bonnie. We were at Carla's beach house. It was the night before Megan drowned. Megan and I stood at the top of the stairs. The audience was seated below on the couch, drinking wine, eating cheese and crackers. Bonnie sucked her thumb, wearing her red-footed pajamas, giggling at us. The piano was pushed into the middle of the room. Megan had the giggles too; I poked her to be quiet. We came down the steps, me in front, Megan right behind me, her hands over her mouth. I announced, "Anna and Megan Levy will now perform 'Beauty and the Beast,' 'Let's Fall in Love,' and, with Carolyn Levy, 'Scarborough Fair.'" Our audience applauded.

Although our playing had improved greatly over the summer, Megan still improvised the low parts of the Beast, mostly by pounding away. This song was all piano, no lyrics, but during my solos, Megan stood and acted out the story, being demure and coy, making turns in her dress for Beauty, and flashing scary faces, holding her gnarled hands up above her head for the Beast. Then she would rush over to hide her face in Mom's lap, running back to the piano for her part.

I did all of the piano for "Let's Fall in Love," booming out,

"Birds!"

Megan chimed in, "Do it."

"Bees"

"Do it"

"Let's"

"Do it"

"Let's fall in love," I cheered.

We performed the whole song. I sang all the verses. Megan had only the chorus of "Do it." And when she forgot to say it, Dad screamed it out for her with gusto.

When we finished, my mother rose from the couch and leaned next to the piano. Megan sat on the bench with me. I did all the playing. Megan and I sang only the chorus, my mother singing the verses alone. We had been practicing for weeks.

"Are you going to Scarborough Fair?" she implored.

"Parsley, sage, rosemary, and thyme," Megan and I harmonized.

"Remember me to one who lives there. She once was a true love of mine."

Mom asked Carla to make a round with her. They sang the song as they each remembered it, Carla higher and a little bit shallower, my mother deep and true.

Tell her to make me a cambric shirt
Child of the mountain
Sleeps on the will of a clarion call
Catch me a sparrow with snow-crested crown
Tell her to find me an acre of land
Between the salt waters and the sea strands
Tell her to reap it in a sickle of heather
Sent us to kill
Blazing in scarlet battalions
Long ago forgotten
Then she'll be a true love of mine.

In that moment, hearing her singing, her eyes shining on Megan and me, my mother was the center of our lives. She always was. We orbited around her, Megan and I; my father did too. And we were safe in her arms to explore the world she presented.

Megan's room was at the end of the hall—a small room with one window, a twin bed, and a tiny wood desk. There was a closet without a door. Her dresses hung on hangers; other clothes were piled at the top of the closet. Those things—and her—were all that fit in her room. She liked that room better than my bigger, brighter one. She also liked to sleep with her door closed. Often at night I read to her in her room.

Once I told Megan the room was too small. She said I was wrong. She told me to turn off the light and close the door. I stood by the door, and she turned on the night-light by her bed. Then she slid under the covers, put her head on the pillow, both hands under her cheek. She said, "See, it's perfect." It was. The room was her size.

Lots of people came to give their condolences and food, but most left quickly. Only Uncle Ben and my mother's mother, Lettie, stayed. She and my mother didn't get along, so we rarely spent time with her and I didn't know her very well. There were many white bakery boxes full of cookies, cookies with chocolate or jelly centers, or shaped like half-moons, or with swirls of red and green, or with brown sprinkles. There were also many cakes, and soups and casseroles and lasagnas, so much that things were left out of the refrigerator, on the counter. I spent time opening and closing the bakery boxes, looking at the cookies while the adults talked.

My grandmother was largely ignored by my parents. She raised our shivah sitting to an Orthodox level. When people went out to sit in the backyard and chat and eat the cakes, she shooed them back into the dark living room scornfully. She told my parents that they could not leave the house during the week of shivah. She covered windows and mirrors. She threw away baked goods that were not from the kosher bakery, and the meat lasagna, including the pan. But mostly she indoctrinated me.

She had seven short days to teach me God. How better to teach someone the power of the Almighty than through a death? We sat at the kitchen table while the rest of the adults conversed in the living room.

Grandma Lettie told me the story of how Moses received God's law on the mountain. How lucky he was to be told the way the people should live. I nodded, nibbling at the cookies she doled out to me on a small saucer, one dish she figured we couldn't have made nonkosher. But I didn't listen to the stories. Her words knocked around me like the checkers we played, hitting the hardness of the board. I didn't absorb any of them. She patted me roughly on the side of my head, like affection but really trying to get my attention. She asked, "Do you remember the Passover you had in my house? You asked the four questions, you were the youngest." I did look up from my plate then, my finger pressed down in the crumbs. Was she trying to please me, because now I was the youngest again?

I had noticed in these days of sitting shivah that no children came to our house. Parents do not bring their children to mourn the death of a child.

My father eventually came along and rescued me from Lettie, saying, "Come Anna, be with us." He put an arm around me and led me into the other room. I felt sorry about my grandmother being treated poorly, ignored and left in the kitchen alone, but I was secretly glad that my parents and I were against her. At least, that I was with them in this one small way; they preferred me. My father sat me on his lap and cradled me against him on the sofa while talking to visitors, but he quickly forgot my presence even while he endured the weight of me against him.

When my grandmother sneaked into the room to pull me back to the kitchen, I felt it was my place to go with her; we were together in our separateness.

One morning my mother came into the kitchen to get away from everyone. She had been sitting with some other teachers from the university, sitting among them but her mind not present. She excused herself and came, practically running, into the kitchen, her hand over her mouth, gagging on her stifled sobs. My grandma was in the bathroom, giving me an unintentional break from my religious education. I was putting a red-stringed box of cookies in the freezer. My mother let go of her mouth and stared, "What are you doing?"

"I'm putting these in the freezer so they don't go stale."

She looked at me for a long moment, and her lip curled up in distaste, then she turned and walked out the door, stepping into the front yard for the first time in days.

Morning is a good time for mourning. I thought of all kinds of ridiculous things following Megan's death. I was eight years old. I liked to examine the words of comfort that adults offered me. The most common reassurance was that things would be back to normal soon. My parents' friends and colleagues wanted things to return to normalcy. They were concerned with the forward motion of their own lives. Adults become shortsighted that way. Children and the dead can see in both directions.

I knew, maybe before she was even dead, while I watched them wrestle with the water, this was a realigning of the planet. The world would sit in a new position. Heat would be hotter, water would boil at a new temperature.

My mother didn't leave the house, afraid to run into people, afraid to see herself out in the world, her arms free of Megan. One night I heard my father shout, "Carolyn, we left her! We couldn't find her and we left!" I stood in the hall outside their door. I heard my father crying like a child. "God help me," he kept saying. I went back to my room. We would leave Massachusetts.

Carla drove us to the airport; we were leaving Boston for California. My mother and Carla sat up front, both staring out the windshield. I was riding in the back with my father. He absentmindedly played with my ponytail. For the past week he had been my link to my mother and to our future.

My mother organized, arranged, packed. My father talked. I listened and followed. My father had told me what we'd do in Berkeley, where we'd stay, who we would meet and spend time with. He told me how we'd feel better in a new environment.

We drove in silence toward the airport, Megan's absence taking up more room than we possibly could, until my mother said to Carla, "I should have checked with you if Bonnie could use any of Megan's things." There was a long pause before Carla replied, "No, Bonnie doesn't need anything." My mother started her heavy crying. I was mad at

Carla then; I thought my father was mad at Carla too. My mother was mad at herself, a habit that never went away.

In the weeks leading up to the move, Carla helped pack our entire house. There was a Noah's ark full of little stuffed cushion animals in pairs and a man and a woman. A Harrods rocking horse with a real horsehair mane and tail, a brand new raincoat and rain boots, a tea set for dolls, all given to charity.

I can remember Megan and Bonnie playing with the Noah's ark. They lined up all the pairs of animals, tall giraffes, plump elephants, sheep and lions, waiting in rows to board the ark, crowding in with Noah and his wife. There was just enough room for all of them. Packed tight, the tiny pillow animals held each other upright in the boat and were peaceful. Grandma Lettie had sewn the set, wanting us to enjoy these biblical stories. My mother didn't want to keep it. The real Chinese pot and cup that Megan drank her tea out of, my mother wrapped in newspaper, kept.

I pilfered one thing out of Megan's room, her toy music box. The outside was white lacquer, decorated with vines and flower buds. Inside, a miniature ballerina twirled on a coiled spring. When the lid was open it played a tinny classical song and the ballerina turned. The closed lid held the ballerina pressed down and the music stopped. When I took the music box out of her room, I opened and closed it over and over, eventually pressing the ballerina down with my finger, stopping the music with the box still open. I packed the music box in the bottom of my suitcase.

My mother was an anthropology professor. She met my father while teaching precolonial African cultures at Harvard. When she joined the anthropology department at Berkeley after Megan died, she taught on African independence, neopolitical structures, economic climates. But her perspective had shifted to a more microlevel, examining the family unit. A human family is easier to study than maintain.

My mother was raised Orthodox. When she and her brother, Ben, were still toddlers, my grandma Lettie thought she was pregnant again. It was a uterine tumor, and she had a hysterectomy. My mother and Ben needed to fulfill all of their parents' aspirations, which would otherwise have been spread out over eight or ten children. They were extremely close. My mom was pushed by her parents to play piano and unwillingly became a concert pianist at ten. Ben assisted her in getting out of it five years later by stepping on her middle finger until it broke. As the finger swelled and turned purple, Ben hid his face in the bed and wept, while she only smiled. Now I have my mother's upright piano in my apartment. I am teaching Adrea to play. Like Megan, Adrea also likes to play the low parts of the Beast; she can better feel the low notes.

In Massachusetts, my father was an educator and a writer working in community health. He was a collaborator on a human sexuality book, a product of the sexual revolution, which was then changing the country's attitudes on sex. This was his sole work in Boston. Once in California, he helped develop the public health department at Berkeley. He was many women's best friend, and he was a feminist.

In Boston, my father's office was a co-op for the book collective. I remember being in the collective's office, lying on the lumpy corduroy couch with Megan. My father and five or six other adults were sitting around the table, talking about being comfortable with the human body. To make his point, my father took off his shirt in a dramatic gesture.

Megan and I began giggling. We burrowed down into the pillows together, hiding from our silly father. We went unnoticed, though, and the other man then took off his shirt to second my father's point, and then the women in the group removed theirs. The six adults stood naked from the waist up.

I wiggled back into the couch cushions to tell Megan about the "nudes." She took one look and jumped up, pulling off her clothes. She danced around the small office, sticking out her ribby, four-year-old chest, and then dove back into the couch to hide.

Everyone laughed.

After several months of staying in faculty housing, we began looking for a house to buy. One day we saw several open houses: one with a round staircase, another with a backyard fishpond, and another with very high ceilings but only one bathroom. I could tell they weren't thinking about Megan that day. But she was with me. I showed her the houses, her room and my room. All the houses we saw had three bedrooms. Were my parents going to make a room for Megan? Admiring the picture windows, they were definitely not thinking about Megan.

I could yell her name out right now in the middle of this empty house. Then they would stop and think about her. Then they would feel bad. We stepped into the backyard with the fishpond; it was murky but miraculously inhabited by large koi fish. As I gazed at the cloudy green water, I imagined Megan reaching for me with her thin arms, the pressure and silence overwhelming her. My dad put his hand on my shoulder. A flash of relief; he was seeing her too. But instead, "So, Anna, you like it?"

By evening I was lost in my head. When they were forgetful, I was the watch guard, my sister's keeper. In the times when my parents became a twosome, trudging forward arm in arm, I brought Megan into the picture. Her small hand tucked in mine, or stealing things from my back pocket, she threw stones and didn't get yelled at, she did her shimmy dances, she tickled me under my arm for attention. It was easy for fantasy to move in on a lonely eight-year-old. Childhood vice of imagination.

That night we went to a lecture on campus. I didn't want to be there, and I felt ignored by my parents and invisible to everyone. I looked around the room as the lecture began; there was nothing for me to do but sit and endure it. I asked my father if he brought me a book or pad to draw on; he just shushed me to be quiet. And then I saw a woman standing to the side of the lecturer, her hands and arms moving fluidly, speaking even through silence; her hands held secret meaning for me. I looked around to see if other people were watching. I noticed I was the only child in the auditorium; I believed the woman was there for me. She was sending me cryptic messages from Megan, silent and powerful. I leaned forward, staring hard at her gliding movements. I knew that was where Megan was, soundless and fluid. Holding my hands cautiously above my lap, I imitated the signs, praying that Megan could hear me.

After the lecture my parents waited in line to talk with the speaker. I lingered around the interpreter. I wanted her to touch me. I wanted to touch her hands. She smiled at me and prepared to leave. I blurted out, "My name's Anna." She said, "Hi, Anna," and smiled again. I paused and then thrust out my hand for her to shake, it was important to me that I touch her hands. She laughed and shook my hand, "Pleased to meet you, Anna," she said. "Thank you," I replied and ducked away.

As we walked up the hill to the faculty housing, I said, "There was a lady onstage, talking with her hands, she may have been talking for Megan."

My mother stopped short and put one hand to her throat. My father put his arm around her and moved her to his other side, away from me. He said, "You mean the sign interpreter?" I felt his dismay. "She translates the speech for the deaf," he explained.

Was he angry? "She was saying things to me too," I insisted. I knew I sounded strange, but I felt certain. I would speak to Megan in that language. I would speak to Megan underwater.

"Anna, please. It's late, it's been a long day; your mother's tired." With one arm still shielding my mother, who was turned away and silent, he stretched out his other hand for me to hold. "Let's go home to bed, okay?"

In the years following Megan's death, my parents developed an inability to fully say no to me. They seemed to consider me equally capable of making good decisions and being in charge, almost as if their right to be parents had been revoked. My decision to pursue sign language was the beginning of this new authority I had over myself.

My father woke me up the next morning saying to come right down for breakfast. I sat at the kitchen table by myself. My father laid out orange juice, scrambled eggs, milk, and toast. He sat down across from me with his coffee cup.

"Mom is staying at a friend's. She'll come home soon." My father's face looked different. His eyes were bulging, with dark circles around them, his skin looked white and dry. He saw me staring and rubbed his eyes and smiled. He looked like a dog showing its teeth.

"Where is she?" I asked.

"Anna, please, eat while it's hot."

Maybe she went home and he didn't want to tell me. Maybe she was back in Boston and I would never see her again.

Then it hit me. She was living somewhere else with Megan. My mom and dad had decided on this; it would be her and Megan, my father and me. Usually I thought I would want to be with him if I could have only one parent. But now I knew the truth; I wanted my mother.

"Who is she with?"

He pushed back from the table. "She's by herself," he said, and stood and walked out, leaving me alone in the kitchen.

The next day when I was alone, I examined their room for things my mother had left behind. I couldn't tell that she had taken anything. I still saw signs of her all around the bathroom, her perfume, jewelry, lavender soap. I even checked the drawer for the blue case of her diaphragm. It made me think maybe my father was wrong and she was coming back today. Or maybe she was getting all new things for her and Megan.

When she didn't come home that night, I observed that her nightgown was missing from the closet and her nighttime face cream was not by the sink. I could imagine the weight of the jar in my hands; I could even smell the cool milkiness of the cream. I found another jar in the medicine cabinet and put it by my bed. Halfway through the week I told my teacher that my mother was gone. She must have called my father, because he came to my classroom and picked me up early. Driving home, he said that he knew they were horrible and he was sorry that I had it so hard. I tried not to listen. I buckled my seat belt; I didn't tell him to buckle his.

The next time my mother was in the house, several weeks later, I heard but did not see her. I had already been asleep and had come back downstairs for some reason. I was dragging my feet over the carpet in the living room toward the kitchen when I heard her voice through the wall. I felt my heart leap in my chest, and I felt like crying. It also occurred to me that it was sad that just the sound of my mother's voice could do this to me.

The wall between the kitchen and living room had a swinging door like a restaurant's. Just outside this door, against the wall in the living room, was a couch. I stretched out there, my head propped on the arm, and listened. I knew they sat at the table, only a foot away from me on the other side of the wall.

I was a harmless eavesdropper because I didn't listen to what was being said. I listened to the tones in which they spoke to each other, the rhythm of their pauses, and the rush of words. I listened for the soft murmurings that my mother hummed with her mouth closed, and the sad sighs my father made. I opened my eyes when the pitch in my mother's voice altered suddenly.

Then came my name and Megan's name, and the words fastened in my brain as though they were my thoughts.

"Remember when Megan was a baby and I said I had more love for Anna?" I heard my mother ask. "I said Anna was more enjoyable."

"Carolyn, that wasn't you. When Megan was only an infant, I said, 'How could I love her as much as Anna?' But we did, we did love her as much."

"But I was always comparing." My mother's voice was monotone. "Anna did everything early, did everything well." She whispered so somebody couldn't hear, somebody, but not me. She didn't think I was nearby, she was whispering for Megan.

I remembered something I'd forgotten then. An evening when my mom was reading me a bedtime story and Megan was a baby, a sitting-up baby who could stand in her crib, holding on, but couldn't walk. Megan woke up and started crying, and my mother kept reading; her voice grew annoyed and we both ignored the crying. Finally I said, "The baby is crying," and my mother said, "It's okay, she doesn't know any better, she should be sleeping." I smiled because my mother was still really my mother and Megan couldn't talk or get up and come to us. It didn't make me happy now, to remember. Now none of us had Megan anymore, and my mother wanted to go away too.

My mother began crying; my father comforted her with soothing sounds. I slid off the couch and crawled across the carpet back upstairs.

One evening shortly after that, while my mother was still away, my father took me to a bookstore on Telegraph Avenue. We separated in the store. I liked being alone in the children's section. I stole glances at girls who were Megan's age, splayed on their mother's lap reading together, or running down the aisle, voices too loud.

I walked around with my hands deep in my sweater pockets, looking but not touching the many books that interested me, until I saw the large hardcover book with photographs of people doing sign language on the cover, *American Sign Language for Children*. I picked it up and found a pillow on the floor to sit on. The book was full of photos of signs, and some illustrations showing the movement to go with the hand shape, and vocabulary words in categories: colors, animals, emotions, greetings, numbers, days of the week. I looked around to make sure no one was watching and I tried some.

I learned the alphabet in about ten minutes and then repeated it three times in a row to make sure I had it memorized. I realized I could talk now if I had to, I could just spell everything. But I was hungry for vocabulary; each new word made me want another, and they seared into my brain. I felt like I would remember them all, they made perfect sense. DOG—snap by knee; HELLO—salute; ENG-LAND—sash of a queen; BOY—pull cap on head; GIRL—tie bonnet under chin! I stopped and took some deep breaths, my heart racing. I looked at my right hand hidden down by the floor and spelled out M-E-G-A-N, HI. I looked up "sister" in the book and tried it with trembling hands.

When my dad returned, I showed him the book. He turned it over in his hands. "You want this?"

"Yes, please," I pleaded. "I've learned a lot, I'm good at it."

My father bought me *American Sign Language for Children*. When I exhausted what the book could teach me, I asked him to sign me up for ASL classes. My mother was still out of the house, and my father had no fight in him. He sighed heavily and said he'd look into it. Every Wednesday night for two hours, my father and I went to class. We faced each other in the classroom, both nervously smiling. I'd point to my chest, make the sign for "name," fingerspell A-N-N-A. Then I'd point at him, make the sign for "name," and squint my eyes, lowered eyebrows, expression of a question. He'd spell out H-O-W-A-R-D. I'd slide my palms across each other, make two fists, index fingers up, bring my hands together, knuckle to knuckle, "Pleased to meet you."

The room was divided by screens. On the other side was an advanced class. We kept hearing laughter seemingly prompted by nothing. For my father and me it was creepy, this unsolicited laughter. A response that comes before the call.

In the next couple of years, after our family was back intact, I took the advanced courses by myself. My father offered to continue, but I knew he didn't really want to. The deaf instructors seemed to make him uncomfortable. He was eager to go home after class to the world of spoken words, telephones, and music, whereas I liked to stay silent as long as possible. I was relieved to learn sign language alone; I wanted privacy.

I befriended a girl with a deaf younger brother. I spent a lot of time at their house. She was my friend, but I always found excuses to involve her brother in our games; we always needed a butler, or warlock, or someone to stay on home base or guard the hidden treasure. I liked watching how my friend could play with, fight with, or ignore her little brother. Their mother kept a close eye on us; she was protective of her deaf child. Her family was something between my family and a normal family. I was more comfortable with them than with other families, families who moved quickly, were loud, who did not think about being careful.

Megan's death was in every molecule surrounding my parents and me, yet nobody said Megan was beyond even silent words. I learned sign language. I wasn't told that death is farther than that. I talked with my hands to my sister, who wasn't deaf but couldn't hear.

My mother was away from us for three months. That time had a lasting effect on me. I saw it as one of the physical stages of our family. I saw our family as sedimentary rock forming over great periods of time. There were layers of time made up of different elements. Each phase was dependent on the previous phase and made the rock itself. First there was the two of them, before I was born, two elements, a base of sandy beige and red clay. Then there were three of us. For a long time, a thick layer of rock formed upward, and it was sandy and red, with glimmering black striations like magnesium. When Megan was born, the next layer became more complex. Maybe there were bits of pink quartz embedded. There were four of us, and the rock looked complete and full. After Megan died, the next layer showed three colors again, but not the same as before. The black shimmerings of magnesium were different; where before they were continuous lines, they were broken up now. And when my mother left for those months, there was yet another layer of time, two colors, for my father and me but blended in a new way. He was an expanse of sand that could hardly hold itself together, and again the shiny black stripes, which were me. When my mother moved back into the house, the last layer formed, three again, sand and red clay and black glimmerings, but not the same as the three elements ever were before. This last layer went on the longest, until I left.

The day after my mom returned home, my father drove me to school. We were silent in the car. My father had an air of strength; I sensed his hopefulness about our improving situation. He sat straight behind the wheel and frequently took in deep audible breaths like affirmations. Despite this, or maybe because of it, I felt lonely.

When he pulled the car up in front of my school, I sat there not opening the door.

"She looks different," I stated, trying to sound merely observant.

My father shut off the engine, put his arm on my seat back. "How so?"

"I don't know."

"Yeah, I suppose she looks a little different. You do too, you look a little older." He smiled at me and squeezed my shoulder.

"Not like that Dad, she looks sort of sick."

He sat and looked at me, a long gentle silence of taking me in. "Anna, between you and me, I don't think your mom is ready to talk about it; she was in the hospital for a short part of her time away. She needed care and rest. She's doing a lot better now, but she still needs our care."

I stared out the car window at my school. I felt like I knew about such things, people going to hospitals when they can't handle life anymore. I'm not a little kid anymore, I thought, if I know about these things.

"I started a new school while she was away. She hasn't even seen this school yet." I started crying, hot tears, but silently, which also made me feel grown-up. "It's not fair!"

My father wrapped his arms around me, smoothed my back. "No, my darling, you're right, its not. There, there," he murmured.

The month after my mother returned, we moved into our new house in Berkeley. Shortly after moving in, my father caught a baby raccoon that was stuck in our attic. He grabbed it inside a big towel and wrapped it up, but it wriggled its head free of the towel and scratched his arms. It finally bit him on the thumb before he got it on the ground and into a metal garbage can and put the lid on. My mother wanted to call an animal shelter to come pick it up and for my dad to go to the doctor. He said he would drive it up to the Berkeley Hills, where it surely came from, and release it. I sat by the can in our narrow side yard while they argued. Why couldn't we just let it loose? Maybe it would stay and live here.

The towel my father used now lay beside the can, and I picked it up. There were long black and gray hairs stuck on it. I fingered them while I listened to the raccoon hissing and screeching inside the can.

I imagined that the raccoon thought it was going to die. I started crying, covering my face with the dirty towel. It smelled wild and musky. I tried talking to the baby raccoon, talking very softly to comfort it. The animal grew quiet for a moment at the sound of my voice and then started up screeching and clawing again. I began crying out loud, overwhelmed by how we were both trapped, feeling miserable just like this wild animal. The raccoon went perfectly quiet when it heard my cries. Even though I was frightened, I lifted the lid of the garbage can to make sure it was alive. The raccoon looked up and blinked at me. I felt like there was a wild animal inside me, and this animal could see that. I felt I shouldn't speak, because my voice would be strange and foreign to the raccoon, who had no language.

We ate dinner together every night. During the meal, both of my parents would inquire about my day at school. I'd report my lessons in each subject, and any special activities or outings I'd done with my class. After dinner, I would do my homework alone in my room. When I was through, I would seek them out again to show them. They never asked to see my homework, and I often felt I was imposing on them for this small attention.

They were usually curled up on the couch together, watching the news or reading. Holding out my few worksheets, I'd say, "I'm finished, you can check it." My mom would smile at me and return to her book or the television. My father was always the one to take the papers, look them over. "Fine job, Anna, very good." They were like a buoy, making an appearance of security but impossible to get a foothold on.

I didn't think we would ever go to the beach again. But a year after Megan's death we solemnly went to see the California coast. We drove across the Bay Bridge into San Francisco. We didn't bring pails and shovels. I sat in the backseat of the car, already in my bathing suit, a yellow terry cloth dress over it. I could see gray water passing by underneath as we drove. When we'd first climbed into the car, left our driveway, we were cheerful in false anticipation. But we never did pretend much, especially when it was just the three of us, and we quickly grew quiet.

We parked, and each carried a bundle toward the shore. I took off my sneakers after we'd already walked a way in the sand, spilling out the fine pebbles. The familiar sensation of my bare feet in the sand made my throat constrict. After laying down our things, my father and I moved forward together. We stepped into the waves, simultaneously stooping to cup the water in our hands.

"It seems colder," I stated in comparison, glancing at my father to see if he approved of my openness in remembering the ocean. It seemed as if he hadn't heard me. He stared out to sea. I followed his gaze. Perhaps from this new perspective Megan would be in plain sight. What if here on Golden Gate Beach sat Megan, patiently filling a pail with sand, waiting for her slow land-bound family to catch up? I looked back at my mother. She was seated in the sand. She had buried her feet and was sifting dry sand through her fingers. She was looking down at her hands, her long brown hair falling over her bent knees.

Suddenly I felt incredibly long legged, giant and unchildlike, as if the ocean could never cover my long pale body from sight. I headed back toward my mother.

She looked up and stared right through me, then turned her gaze down again. I turned back to my father. He still stared out as if the earth might indeed be flat and he could just make out the opposite shore. I felt newly afraid to be near the ocean.

I ran back to him and followed his eyes gazing out to sea. "Is it Massachusetts on the other side?"

"No, come here." He awkwardly picked me up. He was knee-deep in the water. I perched clumsily on his hip, remembering being younger and clinging to his body before I could swim. "The other side is Japan. You realize we haven't seen the ocean in over a year? The beach was my favorite place before Megan died."

I suspected that my father thought I was my mother. I said only, "Put me down."

On the three-year anniversary of Megan's death my mother stayed home sick in bed. My father told me he would go to work, had to get out of the house. My mother slept, and I read through the morning. Every half hour or so, I crept down the hall to look in on her. Her position in bed never changed.

At noon, I was sitting in my room, tracing a map from my geography book, when she suddenly appeared in my doorway. For a moment, in her beige silk nightgown, I thought she was naked. There were tears lining her face. I froze in my desk chair, feeling like there was a ghost in the room. Panting, she said, "I think I have a fever. I keep waking and slipping under again." She sucked air in through her dry lips, new tears falling in the same traces. I looked down at my map, wishing she would disappear.

She came into the room and knelt on the floor by my feet, carefully laying her head in my lap. "Anna, I keep thinking I can see her now. If it were happening now, I could see where she is, pull her out." I looked down at her open mouth, her wet face. I lightly touched her cheek, thinking I was too young to comfort her. There were small baby hairs clinging to her neck, and I combed them with my fingertips. Then I forgot about my distance and the usual numb space between us, and I smoothed her hair back with my flat palm.

For the first time, I saw that I would one day be a woman like she was, full grown, with breasts and long legs, and the kind of skirts and stockings that she wore. For the first time since Megan died, she didn't look unfamiliar and strange to me. She looked like what I would someday be, and I felt as if I were becoming a woman right then.

"It's all right, it's all right," I repeated, listening to the sound of my voice.

She spoke in a calm voice. "Anna, I want to watch the movie, just one time and then never again. I just want to see if I know where she is. I think I know where she is." She lifted her head and looked at me, asking permission.

I knew we still had the movie. My uncle Ben had

watched it, and my father had shown it to Carla and
Mannie once. I would watch it later a handful of times
when I was a teenager, trying to understand what had taken
place. But it did not have any attraction to me then, just
three years after her death, when I could still see the actual
event in my mind's eye.

I set up the projector for my mother, pulled the film
from the spool through the feeder, locked it in place. I
pressed the play lever and moved away from the machine.
I sat on the couch by her feet, half watching, half turned
away.

The black-and-white images were almost nice to see at
first: Carla in her suit pushing the raft out, waving to my
mom, the two girls facing each other, heads down in the
boat. I watched several large waves in the film, not knowing which wave would be the one. Then it came crashing
over the whole inflatable boat, covering the girls. My father
and Carla got their feet under them again. When my father
shoved his hands into the water in bewilderment, realizing
Megan was not within his protective grasp, my mother
crept off the couch and crawled toward the screen. She
looked at the bottom of the frame, the blurred water, flashing light and dark. "I thought I'd forgotten to look here,"
she murmured, "I thought she might be here." My mother
leaned back against the sofa, her hands covering her face as
she cried softly. I stared at her, not the movie, until I heard
it snap off, the finished spool clicking.

My mother climbed up on the couch and hugged me to
her. "Anna, I know you've had a hard time of it. I'm sorry."

My body stiffened, but I hugged her back.

She hugged me closer and cried in my arms.

I woke up early one Sunday morning in Berkeley. I had
just entered my teens, and I felt I was changing all the time,
physically and mentally. The room was very bright and

overheated. On weekends, I was always awake for a while before my parents emerged from their room. Sometimes I made myself something to eat or went outside. Usually I lay in bed though, waiting until I heard them moving around.

I would lie there signing to Megan. I would say, "They're still asleep. Your birthday is coming up. You'd be in the fifth grade, I'm now in eighth." I would sign even my smallest thoughts: the shape of the crack in the ceiling, what it made me think of, how my stomach felt, the kids at my school.

That morning I began signing to Megan about a boy I liked at school. I could not sign, or even say, most of my thoughts. I didn't know how to articulate my feelings lately. I was thinking how alone each person is in their own head, this boy and me, impossibly distant, and my parents and me, like strangers caught in our private thoughts. I was frightened by our separateness, and knowing that I couldn't express my feelings made me feel more lonely.

I stopped signing and slid my hand inside my pajama bottoms. I touched between my legs. I thought, I am thirteen and I have touched a boy and let a boy touch me, and I have kissed full on the mouth, with the tip of my tongue. I opened my mouth, breathing. I licked the back of my hand to feel what my tongue felt like touching somebody.

I opened my eyes and looked out the window from my bed, embarrassed even though I was alone. The sun was bright on the grass, so bright it made the grass look almost white. I squinted my eyes, making the distant mailbox a red dot. I sat up, crossing my legs Indian style, and looked around my room.

I thought, my sister has been dead for five years. I have been the only child for five years. Signing to Megan has always been about my own loneliness.

I didn't sign again that day to Megan and not for the next few weeks either. Although I felt I was discovering the truth that day, I knew I had been pretending for a long time. I hadn't questioned my communicating with Megan through sign; I just talked to her because I needed to. I knew communicating with her wasn't possible. Admitting it made me burn with shame. At thirteen, I decided to face the truth, and in one day I was much older.

My mother paced in circles, took in views, was distracted and distant. In my room, she fingered my schoolbooks, folded stray clothes, absently kissed the top of my head. Drumming her fingers over her lips, or running her fingers over the surfaces, she spoke her thoughts out loud, "Your father chose this bedspread," "I have all those papers to read," "Your hair needs cutting," as she turned in circles from window to window, desk to bed. I avoided her gaze, afraid to trigger her more present mind, which tended toward tears.

My father had begun frequenting bookstores most nights. He was better able to escape his solitude out in public. The house and its narrow yard, the thick-bottomed water glasses, the framed lithographs, the dusty plants, and especially my things, the children things, were accusing.

There were many windows with views. Alone, I pivoted among them. I read, I signed, I took in the view of trees and sky without paying any attention. I thought of the great escape of adulthood when I could get away. I almost always felt alone, but often my mother was right there with me. She would trace her hand down my back while I sat at my desk. Both staring out, unseeing, she would say "Tall Anna" or "My good girl." I hated to think about the meaning of her words.

By fifteen, I had grown aloof from my parents. With my friends I was relaxed and playful, but with my parents and teachers, and to Megan's memory, I grew distant. At the same time that I let go of my diligence in upholding

Megan's memory, my parents regressed in their grief. It frightened me and I tried not to notice.

We were grocery shopping. My parents pushed the cart together, picking their way through the produce. I had gone off to find stoned wheat crackers, marmalade, cherry seltzer, my new teenage delicacies. As I approached our cart, I noticed that I was taller than my mother. I was wearing sandals with a heel, she had flat sneakers. So we're the same height, I thought, and was about to tell her so when my father snapped angrily, "Carolyn, why do you buy artichokes? Nobody eats them."

I pictured dejected-looking artichokes on the bottom shelf of the refrigerator, the pointy leaves bending inward. My mother always tossed them out without her usual comment about waste. I knew who ate artichokes.

"That's not true. Anna likes them."

They both turned to me. My father's face was stretched in a sneer. "Do you, Anna? Do you eat the artichokes?"

I felt a little sorry for my mother, sensing the trap she'd walked into, but mostly I didn't care. "No." I dropped my food into the cart and walked off. I heard her say meekly, "I won't get them."

Driving home I said, "Mom, I'm as tall as you are now."

She grabbed at the opportunity for a harmless subject. "I guess you'll be even taller. I don't think you're done growing. You know, your father grew in college."

It was an unconscious attempt at reconciliation. Nothing had happened, perhaps nothing could clear it up. I looked at my father, shoulders hunched in the passenger seat. He stared out his window. I could see the side of his face, a pulse twitching in his temple. My mother stopped the car at a light, turned on the radio.

He raised his voice above the music. "Megan liked artichokes! Don't you remember? She's the one who ate artichokes! But it wasn't artichokes, it was butter. The child loved butter!" He turned to stare at my mother, his face straining red.

"Please, Howard."

"Go, it's green," he barked, turning back to his window.

I moved to the edge of my seat, behind my mother, anxious to escape the car. When Megan was alive we would always sit in the backseat together, our parents up front. I used to imagine an accident that could happen that would sever the car in one of two ways, either the back from the front, leaving Megan and me parentless, or lengthwise, dividing each child with one parent. I tried to always sit behind whichever parent I liked more at the time, sometimes making Megan switch seats with me during the ride.

On that day, looking at the back of their heads, I wondered how the car could be split three ways.

I helped my mother unpack the groceries, and my father went out for a walk. He had made her cry and he didn't apologize. She was sniffling while she filled the vegetable drawer, placed each egg in the compartment. The egg that seemed to intentionally leap from her hand, breaking on the floor, released her tears. "He's right, you know," she said to me, wiping her running nose with her hand.

"So what? Who cares what you buy?" I said protectively.

She stopped crying with discipline. She began folding the brown paper bags.

"I'll be upstairs, okay?" I ran up the stairs, closed my door, and turned on the radio. I had a job that summer as a counselor at a Deaf summer camp. I was fluent in sign, and I loved playing games and sports with the deaf children, looking after them. I wished it were Monday and I was at camp. I turned the volume down when I heard the front door shut. They started shouting almost immediately. I was surprised; I hadn't thought my mother was angry.

"Carolyn, pay attention to what you're doing." My father patronized. "It's not good for you to go on like this."

"It's some damned vegetables," she protested. "I don't think I was hurting anybody. You're awfully critical of my behavior, what about you?"

"What did I do? I'm not buying food for our daughter who's been dead seven years!"

"I'm not a crazy person. I thought Anna ate them."

"Don't use Anna! Admit what you're doing."

"You're not making any sense, listen to yourself. Why don't you go out for another walk, or sit in a bookstore all night. You're the one who stayed home for a year while I supported this family."

"Some family." He took her advice and walked back out the front door.

I turned the radio back up, louder than before. "Some family." How would he know? He was so selfish. He was right, though; we were all selfish. A family of individuals, giving to the one person who was gone.

When I first left my parents' home to go back East to Columbia for college, it was an immense relief to be truly alone. For the first time there was no longer a missing sister in my periphery. I was just alone. Everything was new and everything was missing. But gradually, separated from home, Megan's little self came back to me. Like the first human emotion of being born, she came back to me angry.

I saw her small bent back turned away from me. She lay on the floor outside my bedroom. So many years later, I could not remember what I had done. Perhaps I had upset her by not letting her play with me. She waited outside, curled on the floor without a shirt, holding her own knees, her back to the door.

If I could turn back the clock now, if nature could reel one of its storms back in, if the ocean could rush inward, turning to a drop of water, then I could go back to that moment, and at the sight of the backside of her, my sister, I could kneel down and embrace her.

What finally enabled me to separate from my parents was discovering sex. When I first felt the solemn intimacy of romantic love, I didn't miss my mother's love. I met Pablo in my first year of college, and I eagerly gave up childhood.

I opened my eyes. I could just see Pablo in the light from the street, sitting on my roommate's bed. He was unlacing his boots. "Anna, can I sleep here?"

"Yeah," I said, closing my eyes again. "Did everyone go home?"

"Yeah, it's late. It snowed."

"I know, I saw that."

I looked at Pablo in the near darkness. He was standing next to the other bed, barefoot, with the rest of his clothes still on. He lived in the same dorm, down the hall. I moved over in my bed and pulled back the covers without saying anything. He walked over and sat on the edge of my bed. He touched my hair tentatively, and then stroked it. I still didn't speak.

Then I had to sit up suddenly. I covered my breasts with my arms. "I think I'm sick."

He quickly lifted up the window above my head. "You want me to take you to the bathroom?"

"No, just the air." I sat there resting against the wall. I must have fallen back asleep.

"Anna, it's cold. You should get under the covers."

I opened my eyes, momentarily rejuvenated. "I have to get some water." I got up and, realizing I was naked, grabbed a towel and went to the bathroom.

I came back with a cup of water, drank half, and handed it to Pablo. Then we got under the covers together. Once in bed, Pablo took off his jeans, leaving on his shirt and underwear. I fell asleep with Pablo's back pressed against mine in the narrow bed.

It was as a friend that Pablo had first come to me, after an undeliberate evening of tequila and sudden snow, our first night together, like two rabbits warm in the ground. The whole next day we stayed in bed. We discovered he was exactly nine months older than me. I said the day he was born was the day I was conceived. He learned the design of my face. Eventually we made love in the sober light.

The summer after my first year of college was the last time I lived at home. I flew back to Berkeley, leaving my clothes and books and stereo with Pablo. I had acquired very little in my first independent year. Pablo would be visiting at the end of the summer, and we would take a road trip through northern California. The night before leaving New York I told him about Megan. It was a major sacrifice, giving up his ignorance. I felt I was giving up the new clean identity I'd forged.

When Pablo arrived in Berkeley, my parents seemed to like him immediately. My mother was particularly accepting of him. Fifteen minutes after meeting Pablo, she whispered to me, "He's lovely, Anna." When he asked where he could put his things, she directed him to my bedroom. She wanted me to be happy, but I also understood that she could be relieved of me.

Pablo said if he hadn't known about Megan, after spending this time with my parents, he would have thought something was the matter with me. They liked him a little too much. As it was, he began to wonder what favor he was doing them by making me happy. It was the last time I stayed in that house with them.

When we left in our packed-up rental car, ready to tour northern California, I buckled myself into the passenger seat and asked Pablo to drive fast. The wind rushed in the windows as we moved mile after mile away from my family home; I was grateful to be going.

I declared my major at the start of my second year, teaching, specializing in Deaf education. I didn't go home again, instead taking New York internships each summer at Deaf schools. In the three remaining years of college, I didn't see my mother at all. My father used to call me once a month on a Sunday. After inquiring about all parts of my life and filling me in on any changes in theirs, he would uncertainly say, "Let me see if your mother is around." Sometimes we would speak briefly then. She might say, "Did your father tell you about our trip . . ." or any other recent event that occurred. I would say, "Yes, he told me," or I might lie and say no and she would say, "Well it was very nice . . . ," and always ending with, "Well then, take care of yourself, Anna."

"Yes, I will." But sometimes there was already a dial tone. She ended conversations with me with the one sentiment she had longed to impart many years ago.

I learned to get off the phone with my father before he could summon my mother.

After graduation I traveled alone to France for the summer, the trip a present from my parents. I wanted to travel alone, but I asked Pablo to create my itinerary with me. On my last day in France, before traveling inland to Switzerland, I drove to the beach at La Rochelle. I was not prepared to see its gray-blue face. I wanted to laugh at my own silliness in caring that it was that ocean. I'd swum at the beach, but this was the first time I'd been near the Atlantic again.

Looking out at the eastern shore of that ocean, I remembered when I first saw the Pacific at nine years old. I had wondered if Megan could have turned up there. Then, I had imagined the Megan who was still fresh in my memory, five years old, having run ahead and gotten lost.

As a young woman on that European beach, I again played a fleeting mind game. Megan could have arrived here. She'd be eighteen. She'd remember nothing of her life. I pictured a beautiful mermaid emerging from the waves, starting a new life.

I began to cry. Since I was eight years old all of my tears had come from this same body of water. Megan's death had obstructed almost every other pain. I only allowed myself to grieve this one thing. A grown woman, angry that her tears are salty as the sea.

BOOK THREE

My father asked if he could come out to see us for a weekend before we left for France.

"Just you, not Mom?" I had not seen her in almost two years. She'd met Adrea only once.

Surprised by my inquiry, he said, "Well, she thinks you'll be busy. Will you be too busy for me to come?"

"No, Dad. If we have things to do you can help, please come, you can both come." When he called back it was clear it would be only him.

The buzzer rang after 11:00 P.M. My father carried his one small bag up the three flights of stairs.

We sat at the kitchen table, having tea and cookies.

"She must be sleeping already?" he said.

"She couldn't stay up. She made you a drawing; I think it's in her room."

He was looking at Adrea's new passport. "She's grown a lot, very pretty."

I thought that if she were my natural child, his biological granddaughter, he would have gone to take a peek at her sleeping. But it didn't seem to occur to him. He didn't think of her as his in any way. I sat down next to him, consciously trying to stop my expectations.

He rubbed the back of my hand, resting on the table. "So, this is a big deal, this trip. She could really learn to talk?"

I shrugged, not sure I felt like getting into it. "Not fluently or anything. Deaf who use hearing aids can learn to talk pretty well; they can hear a certain amount. She doesn't have any hearing, but she could still use her voice to some extent to communicate, she can learn how to lip-read."

"That seems so difficult to me, lip-reading. I find it quite amazing." He scratched his forehead, the way he always did, lowering his face down to his hand, elbow on the table. "Sign isn't based on English, right? I mean she only knows English from reading."

"That's right." I was happily surprised by his knowledge.

In the living room he showed me some magazines he'd brought. He'd been writing articles and editorial letters on education and public health for different journals. We sat on the couch, reading the magazines.

"Your writing is less idealistic," I observed.

He laughed. "I know more about life's limitations."

I closed the journal and handed it back to him. "Is Mom all right?"

"Fine, she's fine. I brought some pictures from Napa. It was beautiful."

"You go there every year."

He laughed again. "Well, we know we like it."

He reached into his briefcase and took out an envelope of photographs. There were several pictures of my mother but all from a distance, showing off the vast landscapes, shrunken thwarted-looking grapevines. She looked young and small in blue jeans and a hooded sweater. One picture was a close-up. She was sitting at a wooden picnic table under an arbor, her back to the camera. Her hand was resting on the table, next to a bottle of wine. The sun was making watery shadows across her body. I studied her hand. It looked just like my own. I passed the picture back to my father. We made the couch up for him to sleep on. When we said good night, he embraced me, saying, "It's so good to see you," with what sounded like tears in his voice.

Adrea stood beside the couch looking down at my father while he slept. I motioned that she should tap him on the shoulder. She poked one small finger into his shoulder and drew her arm away. He turned and moaned a little. She poked him again and he opened his eyes. Adrea signed HELLO, a hand waved from the center of the forehead. He gave her a groggy smile and reached out to hug her. She let him embrace her but turned her face to look at me. When he let go she pulled the covers off him and ran over to me, ducking behind me.

"Somebody's ready for you to get up, I think."

"Somebody very persuasive," he said, sitting up. He wiped his mouth and signed, "How are you?" with a little hesitation.

She signed O-K, the two letters, which was a new thing for her. He looked confused, and she did it again with both hands this time. Still having no luck, she signed GOOD.

He stood up and stretched out his arms. To my surprise, Adrea went over and gave him another hug. He bent down and closed his eyes, saying, "Oh, sweet baby."

Over the weekend Adrea and my father played Go Fish and Old Maid, drew pictures, and baked mandel bread. He even played with her in her bath. When he signed I LOVE YOU, she signed it back. He spoiled her with presents, a giant panda bear and a purple fleece jacket for France. We went to the natural history museum and the Native

American museum downtown. Maritza babysat Saturday night, and my father took me to the theater. We tucked her in before going out. My father perched on her bed while I stood by the door. He pressed the blanket underneath her body from head to toe, making a mummy out of her. Adrea giggled the whole time. I was seeing my father play the same game with Megan. My father removed a velvet bag from his pocket and put it on top of Adrea's chest. She worked one arm out from under the blanket, "For me?"

My father nodded. Adrea sat up and turned the bag upside down, dumping gold and silver marbles onto the bed. She stirred them with one finger. "Are they real?"

My father looked to me to translate. "Real what?" he replied.

"Gold and silver!" Again, I translated.

"They're special marbles, angel, like you." Adrea carefully put them back in the sack and hugged my father.

We were both sad to see him go on Sunday night, and Adrea talked about him for several days afterward. The last thing he said when we hugged good-bye was "Your mother should have come." It brought the image of that photograph into my mind, her blurred back turned away.

There was a surprise bon voyage party at the Hearing Center. The party started at three o'clock, when the after-school children arrived. Maritza bought mostly French dishes, not so much for Adrea or me, but so the kids could all get a taste of what we would be experiencing. There was a chocolate soufflé, mushroom and spinach quiches, French bread and Brie cheese, and other pastries that I suspected were from an Italian bakery.

Maritza gave each of us a journal "from the kids," and she had bought Adrea a small automatic camera, her first. There isn't a better going-away present for a deaf child.

As the party dwindled down into a regular school day, I

sat with Maritza drinking coffee and feeling homesick already. Adrea came over and slung her arm around Maritza's shoulders, leaning into her. Maritza asked her, "Will you want to come home to us after learning in a French school?" Adrea knocked the air in the sign for "yes," a greater commitment than just nodding her head.

She signed, "When we come home, we can show everyone our journals so they'll know everything we did."

I smiled, signing, "What if you write things that are private that you don't want other people to read?"

She tilted her head, thinking about the possibility of something private. Maritza stroked Adrea's head. Adrea's face grew serious; she asked, "What will we do that I won't want anyone to read?"

"I don't mean anything bad, just maybe something private, only for you to remember."

O-K. She pulled away and ran over to join the group on the rug for story time.

Maritza and I began clearing up from the party, and it occurred to me that for weeks we had not spoken much about the trip. I said, "It's exciting, the trip, the program."

Maritza dumped a stack of dirty paper plates in the garbage. She wiped her hands on her legs and looked at me. "Yes, it is. You know, you don't need my approval."

I looked at her with hurt and surprise. "I'm not trying . . . I thought maybe I haven't been talking to you because it's complicated, I haven't known how to talk to you." I glanced around the classroom. "This obviously isn't the best time." I continued clearing the leftover party food.

"You do seek outside approval." Maritza also looked around to make sure we were alone. "Before you adopted Adrea I honestly didn't know if you should. I thought maybe it would be better for her to be raised by a deaf parent. But something happened between the two of you. Now I think it's for the best."

"I think this trip will be good for her too," I said.

"Good, then trust your own judgment." She began wiping the table with a sponge. I went upstairs to my office.

Adrea asked me if flying through the clouds made any noise. I told her that we don't hear anything outside the plane except the sound of the engine. She frowned at me and turned back to the oval window. Her body bounced at the sight of a billowy puff brushing against the metal body of the plane.

I watched the back of her head excitedly turning left and right, looking down at the square shapes of land, so much like a map, and at the billowy mist blowing by. When we punctured the cloud ceiling and leveled out above the solid mass of clouds, Adrea banged her flat palm against the window. She slapped my thigh, trying to share her excitement. "Look, I could walk out there and do somersaults all over the sky." Then she looked at the other passengers around us; some of whom were staring. She signed to me, "All hearing people," and turned back to the window, leaving one of her sturdy hands pressed into my lap.

As soon as we stepped outside the airport, I saw the school's minibus that I had been told to look for. I realized how little I knew in advance about what to expect. We climbed into the vehicle, handing the driver our papers, just smiling, feeling silly. I do not speak French, so in some ways I would function as a deaf person, relying on gestures to communicate. But driving through the city with the windows rolled down, I was aware of one of the biggest parts of traveling, the different sounds. It was alienating and intriguing to hear only French on the street. Adrea was watching everything go by attentively. I looked some more, blocking out all sound, just seeing. It was still new and quite different, but the world felt smaller. I had visited France once before, right after college. I reminisced on my younger self, who had just earned a degree in Deaf education. I had still been shedding the skin of childhood then, seeking my own identity. I was with Pablo then too, but we were both thinking we should explore our adulthood independently. Now we were tentatively coming together again. I felt sorry for all of us struggling humans just trying to figure this life out.

I saw a man in a long raincoat lifting his daughter onto a city bus, a woman buying fruit from a cart, a flood of beeping cars rushing by. These people were not so different from people in New York, when you didn't hear their difference. But then I knew that Adrea was more observant in sight than I was. She would notice particular French things that my eyes skimmed over.

I tapped her on the shoulder several times before she turned to me. "Does it look different?" I asked her.

Sign is a language that loves opposites. You can make a sentence out of a pair of opposites, ugly or beautiful, smart or stupid, married or single? Adrea responded impatiently, "Different? Nothing's the same!" She turned her face back to the window, now looking through the viewfinder of her new camera. I kissed the top of her head, which went ignored. I smiled and watched the city go by too.

We were in the Marais district at Xavier's apartment, the Frenchman we'd met at our interview at Columbia. There were about twenty people sitting on small couches or chairs, or standing in doorways holding plates of food. Adrea and I were seated on a loveseat, our plates filled with food. I held a bowl-size glass of red wine. A few sips made me aware of my exhaustion.

Adrea kept twisting around in my lap to sign random observations to me. "It's dark in here, only candles." "None of the children are playing, just sitting with their parents, right?" "It's a different time in New York right now."

A woman sat in a chair beside us, speaking English with a French accent. She introduced herself with a horselike laugh, telling me that her husband was American and now she finds it easier to befriend Americans than French. It was one of those moments I recognized, in which I was supposed to have a husband. I thought of Pablo, somewhere in Paris right now.

Smiling toward Adrea, she apologized for not knowing sign language and said, "What a magnificent child." Her husband worked for the school and was also hearing. She pointed him out across the room.

Adrea was fully slumped against me, asleep. I took a sip of wine and shifted her weight. When the woman moved off to mingle, Xavier came over to say hello. Here I got my first real practice in French sign, needing to try saying things a few times before getting it right. I felt out of place and couldn't think of the reason for our being in that lovely apartment, in the capital of France, moving our hands in this strange new way.

After Xavier welcomed me, he departed to greet other guests. Adrea seemed to be out for the night. She curled up on her side of the loveseat, hands in loose fists under her chin. She was my familiar doe-child, yet I was still struck by her beauty. I was lonely and dying for sleep. Briefly, I felt I could cry.

A woman knelt down in front of the couch, gently touching my knee. She had the ethereal good looks of a mermaid. She spoke and signed, "My name is Katrice, I'm one of the language instructors at the school. I am looking forward to working with your daughter."

In the dream there is an elderly man carrying a lumpy canvas sack. His face is bristled with gray and black stubble. He wears a black wool cap. I think, ah, yes, he's French. He enters what looks like a barn or a very old house with raw wood walls, dirt floors. He lays down the sack, and I notice a squirming inside the canvas. I had thought it was potatoes. But seeing the bag move, on its own, doesn't frighten me. Perhaps the bag is full of kittens. Suddenly there is nothing I want more than a kitten. The short old man bends over and unties the piece of rope knotting the bag. His back is toward me; I cannot see the bag or what he is doing. He turns and faces me, and in his arms is a horse the size of a foal. It is a red horse with a long wet head. It is motionless. He says, "It's dead." I only nod acceptance, but I am thinking that I just saw it moving.

The dream left me depressed. I sat on my twin bed in the dormitory, my back against the wall, pulling my knees in to myself. Adrea turned and made a whining sound in her sleep. I wondered where her subconscious mind was taking her. I longed for my big bed at home and bringing Adrea in to sleep with me.

Tomorrow she might be making sounds I've never heard before. Tomorrow I may be able to make out the sound of her voice. The dream slipped away from me; I was left with the image of the newborn horse, hanging limp in the man's arms.

I fell back asleep with the thought of calling Pablo in the morning. I was already looking forward to our whole weekend together in Paris at the end of our trip.

The three adjoining classrooms were laid out like a railroad flat, each with several computer stations. There were children already at work, microphones to their mouths, eyes glued to the monitors. We stopped and watched a boy who looked to be Adrea's age. He was breathing strenuously into the microphone, making a Hee . . . Hee sound as he exhaled. On the monitor a large red balloon inflated with each Hee. When he reverted to just blowing air, making no sound, the balloon started shrinking. A teacher nudged him in the back; he took a deep breath and went back to his one-syllable tirade. I signed to Adrea that he was making one sound that made the balloon blow up. I didn't know the proper way to explain the exercise. I could see she was interested in trying, but nervous she couldn't do it.

The teacher who was working with the boy took Adrea's hand and put it in front of her own mouth. Then she made the Hee sound like the boy. Adrea made a move to pull her hand away, but the woman held tight. I realized how pressured she would be in this environment. The teacher repeated the sound over and over again, exhaling her warm breath onto Adrea's hand. Then she actually took Adrea's fingers and traced them over her lips, to show her the shape the mouth needs to take. She placed Adrea's hand on her own lips, asking her to imitate the expression. By each computer was a mirror. The teacher pointed Adrea toward a mirror. Adrea made the same face and then exhaled without making any sound. The teacher took her hand back and made the sound again on her fingertips with extra emphasis and force. Adrea tried again, making a different sort of breathing sound like panting, but not anywhere near the Hee, Hee sound that the red balloon demanded. The teacher praised her effort and told her that they'd try again later with the headphones. Adrea nodded and showed a weak smile. I knew they would be testing whether she had any degree of hearing. I imagined that she was remembering our one visit to the specialist in New York. Her back flat on the examining table, eyes shut tight.

We saw Katrice working with a girl on another computer. There were rows of train tracks back and forth across the screen. An old-fashioned steam engine moved down the tracks and blew smoke if the girl could say Choo . . . Choo into the microphone. It was the same concept as the first computer, a more difficult word sound. We watched admiringly as the girl called out the command. Again I described to Adrea that the girl was making the sound of a train whistle. She nodded impatiently, already understanding that much.

When the girl put down the microphone, Adrea tapped her and signed YOU'RE GOOD. Katrice gave Adrea a huge smile and tugged a piece of her hair. Adrea blushed with pleasure, looking at Katrice with a shy attraction. I was reminded of Maritza saying that something had already occurred between Adrea and me; remembering my need for her approval saddened me.

Katrice introduced herself to Adrea and said, "I saw you last night, sleeping at the party. You are very beautiful." The French sign was different, and Adrea indicated that she didn't understand. They experimented, signing until they understood each other.

Adrea signed, "I think you're beautiful," then ducked her head behind me in embarrassment.

Katrice laughed and signed, "Then we've agreed to be secret admirers, except we didn't keep the secret." "Secret admirers" she signed also in ASL, and her facial expression and gestures were so intrinsically human we understood her full meaning.

Katrice led Adrea to a nearby table to show her another computer program. Adrea happily took her hand and followed her away from me. If the learning was going to be challenging and even painful, I figured Katrice's affection would help Adrea through it.

Adrea stopped at the next workstation; I stood behind her and Katrice. I recognized by her posture that she was intimidated. This computer was a maze, like a Pac-man game with little rewards of gold coins and colorful fruits in the corners of the maze. However instead of a Pac-man was a little plus sign like a compass, with north labeled as the vowel "O," south as "A," west as "U," and east as "E." When the student pronounced each vowel, the lettered plus sign would move around the maze in that direction. A boy who appeared to be the oldest child was currently using the computer at a steady slow pace. He was trying to move the plus sign down toward a purple bunch of grapes, but instead it kept moving toward the right because he was making a long Ee sound by mistake. I bent around to see Adrea's expression. She had no understanding of how it worked. The teacher pried one of the boy's hands off the microphone and put it on her lips, shouting Ay, Ay, Ay, Ay. She put her mouth right up to his ear and continued shouting. Suddenly the boy changed vowels, and the plus sign jumped down to gobble the grapes.

It appeared that most of the children were wearing at least one hearing aid.

There was a major difference in the teaching techniques from what we do in the States. On the first day of school at home all of the children would be new. The class would be taught with the expectation that they were all at the same level. Here, on the first day they have older students already familiar with the material and the exercises doing what the new students will be learning, tiered learning. The new students learn by observing more advanced children, just as all children learn to play and socialize by watching each other. The experienced children also learn more by teaching and demonstrating to the new kids. We wandered through the school like an open house, seeing the successes and failures. When Adrea left my side to trail Katrice and the other children, it was like the irresistible pull of a school of fish showing her which direction to swim.

Our second night in Paris we walked around the city with Pablo. We stopped in a café for something to drink. I asked Adrea if she wanted juice, but she shook her head, wanting to try something new. Pablo ordered her a *limonade* soda that came in a tiny green bottle, like a huge beetle.

She cradled the green glass in her hands like a jewel, making a face of awed appreciation, displaying her find to us.

"I lived in this neighborhood as a boy, after my parents divorced," Pablo said, stopping to order us some port. "I was teased in school for being named after Picasso. My mother saved me by telling me to use my middle name. She also insisted I keep my father's name, Wilkes; she said it was only a temporary separation, and after all I was still his son. I had this old American last name, a Spanish first name, no father, and called myself Remy, which I didn't answer to."

Pablo took a swallow out of his tiny wineglass. I'd heard this story before, but tonight it struck me in a new way. I contemplated our very different upbringings, and what it must have been like for him to grow up as the center of his mother's universe.

Pablo continued, "The funny thing is we lived in Paris alone until I was ten, and then she was right; we moved back to New York and they remarried. He had separated from his other wife." There was a degree of admiration for his mother written on his face. Pablo looked at me; I don't know what he saw in my expression, but he said, "Then I was an outsider in their rekindled relationship. Like you— I never thought of that." Pablo leaned over and kissed the side of my head in my hair. Adrea glanced at us cautiously. I sipped the sweet wine and held it in my mouth.

Pablo pointed out to Adrea a lapdog sitting at the table next to ours. Then he made a mimed gesture, rubbing his stomach, saying, "Are you hungry?"

Adrea showed him the sign for "hungry," then looked at me and signed, "What time is it?" I smiled at what seemed like an adult concern to eat at the right time. I told her, "We have jet lag from the time being different here. It's dinner time."

Persistent as the little prince, she repeated, "What time is it?"

Out on the street, we began walking, and Pablo draped his arm around my shoulders. I watched our reflection in the shop windows.

I took Adrea up to the classroom we'd explored the previous day. A teacher came striding over and said in English, "Only Adrea today, you're on your own." He signed the same thing in French sign, taking off to greet other new students.

Adrea gripped my hand, looking at all the strangers around the room. I knew that she didn't understand the French sign and wasn't aware I'd be leaving her. Another teacher called out to me from across the room, "Time to go." I looked around for Katrice. I would have liked to leave Adrea, like a young starfish, reattached to Katrice's hand. She wasn't there.

"Adrea, they only want the children here today, no parents. I have to leave now." Her eyebrows furrowed, and she looked around the room again. She let go of my hand and started squeezing her own hands together in tight fists.

Before I adopted Adrea, when I would take her back to Mrs. Carter's house after a day at the Hearing Center, she would often do that with her hands. I cringed to see her making that same gesture. She turned back to look at me, and I saw in her panicked eyes that she wasn't ready. Her small fingers were so tense she could hardly sign. Her signs came out staggering, painfully. "I don't want to learn how to speak. I want to go home with you. I can't speak." Tears tipped from her eyes, and she wiped them away angrily. "Why did you bring me here?" she accused. Her eyes were focused in the distance, not looking at me; I suspected being angry at me was as frightening as being there.

I got down on my knees and stroked her hair down the sides of her face. "I know this is scary. I'm not going to make you do anything. You don't ever have to speak, but we came all the way over here—"

Adrea pushed my hands away; she snarled at me, her lips curling, and a new sound, a frustrated, trapped, wild animal sound escaped her. I had a flash image of a baby raccoon inside a metal can. And then she was down on the floor, curled with her head hidden in her arms. When I touched her leg she kicked me. I picked her up and tried to stand her on her feet, but she kicked me again and collapsed to the floor.

Katrice appeared and, kneeling down, signed to Adrea, "It's all right. We're going to teach you some new games. Nothing bad, you're going to draw on the computer just like with crayons and paper. I'll be here too and we will eat lunch together. Okay?"

Adrea nodded, tears hanging from her lashes. She allowed Katrice to lead her into the group. Then Katrice pulled me out the door, closing it behind us. "She's going to be fine, Anna, this is her first lesson." I looked at her blankly, ready to go back into the room and get my child. "She's okay," Katrice continued, "already she is playing with the other children, I know."

I tried to respond calmly, "Maybe this is too difficult for her and not even right."

"You feel guilty about Adrea's having this challenge?"

"I may have made a mistake, bringing us here."

"No, it's not a mistake for her. Deaf children are strong."

I looked back at her, suspecting she was questioning how strong I was.

Adrea's face was pale, surrounded by a circus of hair. Her first day accomplished, her eyes were tired and happy, like an athlete after training, winding down but still in motion.

When she saw me she smiled placidly, not a glimmer of the child who usually runs unabashed to greet me. She walked up to me, papers in hand, and showed me the computer drawings she'd made, one with crayon and then a computer replication. Another page of print in her handwriting had the word sounds Shh, Choo, Ahh, Mmm, on down the page. I signed to her how impressed I was, how much hard work she'd done today. When I opened my arms asking for a hug, she moved into them heavily, rested against me.

We gathered ourselves to leave. Adrea made a circle of the room, saying good-bye to each student and teacher. We headed out into another night in the foreign city. Standing outside the school, holding Adrea's hand, I thought, she has no idea I'm as lost and unknowing as she is.

My next few days were spent alone. I told Adrea, "I'm also walking around wondering about Antoine de Saint-Exupéry." I walked the narrow streets, people-watching. Stopping at the same place almost every day for a croissant and coffee, I took pleasure in being recognized in a foreign place. The Musée d'Orsay was my favorite place to go. The museum was built inside an old train station. It was a small museum, all nineteenth-century art. I looked at every painting there, but the café was my favorite part. One wall of the café was the giant clock that was the prominent front of the museum's exterior. I always sat in front of the win-dowed clock, feeling it as a giant eye peering out on the city and in over the people. It was an eye and a clock, a symbol to me of our random placement in time and space. The clock goes on as the sun continues to burn and the planets rotate around it and the moon turns around the earth, and of course the tide, ebbing and flowing, regardless of man. But man cannot at all act without regard to any of this.

In front of the clock, I remembered the dream from my first night in Paris. I knew that the foal in the sack had been alive, the wet matted fur, a hard sweat turned cold. But when the old man said it was dead, I accepted that. I agreed to its death too quickly. I could have objected, shouted at him, "You're wrong, it's alive!" And surely in a dream, a voice or action can resurrect a dead thing. But in the dream I knew it was the truth when he spoke it. I knew that regardless of what I wished, whatever was right and fair and just, the way things should have been—the omnipotent force of the universe cannot be argued with. I knew the old man's words were true. It was dead, even if it had been alive a moment ago.

"Should we call Bonnie, see how she's doing?"

Adrea closed her workbook and jumped off her side of the makeshift double bed. We had pushed our twin beds together in our dorm room. And to make the place more homey we'd taped up Adrea's drawings and pictures bought on the street or torn from French magazines. We filled a couple of empty wine bottles with fresh flowers too.

Adrea leaned against my chair while I proceeded through the complicated process of making an international phone call. Halfway through I was disconnected and started again. Adrea signed, "Did you talk to her? She's not home?"

"I'm still trying, there's lots of numbers." Finally I heard a dusty-sounding ring. I imagined her phone bleating out in the dark somewhere. Bonnie picked up, her voice clear and loud as if she were in the room. Suddenly I felt extremely lonely. I nodded my head up and down, grinning at Adrea.

"Bonnie, it's us. How are you?"

"Hey! I've been waiting for you to call, I didn't know how to reach you guys." She jumbled her words excitedly. "Oh, screw it, I had all these funny ways to tell you but I can't think; we're having twins!"

"Twins? Oh my God, hold on, let me tell Adrea." I signed, "Bonnie is going to have twins, two babies are in her belly."

Adrea jumped up and down, making a dance out of the number two. Normally when I'm on the phone and Adrea is interested, she'll wander off and wait until I'm done to ask me what happened. But this time she urged me to continue talking and stood by my arm, watching my lips, waiting. I wondered if it was because it was a special call, away from home, or because she was learning to lip-read.

"Are there any twins in your family?"

"There are now, Simon's family has some. I'm so tired."

"Oh, it's wonderful, Bonnie."

"I feel them moving, I imagine they're playing with each other." She paused for a breath I could hear across the phone wires.

"How's Simon? Are you two playing nicely?"

"Yeah." Bonnie laughed. "We're good. So when are you coming back?"

"Four and a half weeks, we'll come see you," I promised.

"How's Adrea? How's she doing with it all?"

"She's great—I don't really know. They keep the parents pretty much out of it. It's kind of hard being here; I'll tell you about it when we're back."

"Okay. Hey, ask Adrea what I should name these babies."

Adrea considered the question very seriously, then asked, "Will they be girls?"

"We don't know yet."

While Adrea was thinking I told Bonnie her question. Bonnie said they would wait to see. Adrea tapped me on the arm, signed slowly, M-A-D-E-L-I-N-E, "if there's a girl." We had been reading the Madeline books.

We talked for a short time, and for the rest of the evening I thought of the clock, the cafés, the speech computers, Pablo, all of the things I wanted to tell her.

At the end of our second week, I came into Adrea's class a few minutes early to pick her up. Taking the seat nearest the door, I watched the kids finishing their lesson. They were playing an animal charades game. A picture of a cow was up against the blackboard. The kids began circling around on the rug, pawing the floor, turning their pinkies up on the sides of their heads for horns. The teacher stomped the floor and signed and said, "Who knows the sound a cow makes?" All the children raised their hands. The teacher pointed to one boy, who walked up to the chalkboard and wrote "Moo." The teacher nodded and looked around the room, pointing to each child, eyebrows raised. Each child, including Adrea, made the sign of agreement. The teacher led them through the same process with a cat, dog, pig, sheep, and duck. Then the children were all assigned a particular animal, and again they circled around the room, imitating their animal in body movement. Adrea was the cow. She waved at me on her way by in the circle. They were asked to stop eventually, and they signed the whole barnyard in French sign. I practiced the new signs as well.

Then the teacher knelt down, saying loudly to one boy, the sheep, "Baa," placing his fingers on her lips. Then she turned his fingers to his own lips. The boy imitated her, "Boo," and after a few more attempts, "Baa." I sat up in my chair, wondering if Adrea would do the same. While the teacher worked her way down the line of children, I watched Adrea. She hopped back and forth on her feet, watching her classmates, relaxed and smiling. Her smile would broaden and she would nod when her classmates got it right and the teacher moved on to the next student. The teacher came around and knelt in front of Adrea, asking her, "What is the sound the cow makes?"

Adrea fingerspelled M-O-O. She put her fists to her temples and smiling, she turned her hands upward, poking her extended pinkies at the ceiling, like horns. In a hoarse, breathy voice, she said, "Moo."

I pitched forward in my seat. Her lips were pursed in a sweet little O shape. She held her mouth for a long time, a smile prickling the corners, unsure if a word had come out. The teacher patted her on top of her head and stepped away. Adrea twisted around to see me. I grinned at her, holding back tears. Adrea giggled; sticking her neck out in my direction, she teased, "Moo." I was consumed by her voice, so husky and honest, it matched everything about her. I said "Moo" back, the mama cow answering her calf.

We went out to dinner with Katrice, Xavier, and Martin. Adrea skipped back and forth between Katrice and me, chattily sharing her impressions and thoughts in a pidgin of American and French sign. Xavier was intent on educating me about Deaf culture in France, or more so, the lack of understanding he perceived from the hearing population. He signed to us in ASL, which was beginning to look odd to me: "I love New York. I spent five years there when I was young and handsome. They are very accepting in New York. Nobody cares what you are, deaf, communist, gay, a drug user; nobody looks twice."

I watched him while I buttered some bread for Adrea. She was pulling on my arm in hungry impatience. I managed to nod at Xavier and reply, "Yes, it's true," taking a second to wonder exactly what he was telling me about himself.

"In America, the parents of deaf children learn sign language, the family adjusts, like your center, for families. Not in France; here the child must adjust, must learn to read lips if he wants to follow along, to be included. The children are sent away to special schools if they are lucky; many are left at orphanages, or worse." He leaned forward aggressively, raising his bushy gray eyebrows at me. I nodded again uncertainly. "If you don't believe me you can ask Katrice."

I looked at Katrice. She had not been following our conversation. She was engaged in conversation with Martin. Xavier frantically waved his hand over the table to interrupt Katrice and Martin and signed. "Please, dear, excuse me, I want Anna to hear about your mother, so she can see how these French are."

She answered him sharply in French sign that her mother was not mistreated because of the way French people are, but because of the way her parents were. She signed that we should wait one minute. I watched her listening to the end of Martin's story, while she combed Adrea's hair through her fingers.

Xavier took Adrea up to the bar with the empty water bottle to trade in for a new one. Katrice turned to me, laying her warm hand down on top of mine. "Xavier is not so strange as he seems. It is very sad to see French families keep their deaf children separate. Especially when he was growing up, they were not accepted. But we both know that's not just France." I understood she was referring to Adrea. Katrice and I had developed a habit of speaking in English when there were no deaf people around. I preferred that intimacy.

Xavier and Adrea returned to the table. He began signing before he even sat down. "My parents didn't even know I was deaf until I was five or six years old! They thought I was quiet and shy. Yes, that was a hundred years ago, but imagine being so unaware."

Katrice continued in pidgin sign, now that Xavier and Adrea were present. "My mother was deaf but was considered retarded by her parents; they never bothered educating her, or even communicating with her. When she was fifteen she became very hard to handle, and they had her committed to an asylum for the insane. She was not able to get herself released for five years. She was mistreated, I mean she was treated as if she were insane."

"More than that," Xavier insisted, "I know your mother."

Adrea sat in my lap, something she hadn't done in a long time. She pulled my arm around her waist, lightly pinching my skin. I lifted my hands up in front of her awkwardly to say something, but Adrea pushed my hands back down and began stroking my arm. The story of Katrice's mother must have been frightening her. I kissed the side of her head, and she sank against me.

Xavier pointed to Martin at the other end of the table. "I could be just like that young man." I looked at him strangely, not understanding. Our soup and salad arrived, and I asked Xavier to excuse my attention for a moment while I situated Adrea on a chair between Katrice and me.

Xavier signed to Martin, "I want you to listen." Martin leaned forward intently, a cigarette dangling from his hand. I could tell from his bright eyes that he'd had a few drinks.

Xavier began, "So, young man, I have a story for you; everyone may get something out of it." He paused to rotate his gaze among our faces, making sure he had everyone's attention. "I have hearing aids too. I can hear quite well with them, and I could have a nice strong voice like our Martin here." Martin watched him with an expression of curiosity that was not without tension.

Adrea was also studying Xavier, her index finger slowly tracing circles around her ear. She knew that she was not like Martin or Xavier.

"When I was thirty-five they put the latest model of hearing aids on me, imagine! They worked, and I was completely lost. Who knew that chairs make noise, that snow doesn't? I had such a headache; I went straight home and took them off."

His words resonated with the feeling gnawing at me since our arrival. Should we be here? Wasn't sign language the natural language of the Deaf? I didn't know the answers. It had been such a long time since I knew for sure what was right or wrong.

We'd been in Paris for four weeks, and our long weekend at Pablo's mother's apartment had arrived. We packed one suitcase and took the *metro* to her neighborhood. Pablo opened the front door wearing an apron, *"Bonjour!"* He gave us a tour of his mother's apartment. The downstairs was a tiny kitchen and a plush living room crowded with knickknacks. Upstairs, we got a peek of the very small guest room he was sleeping in, and then standing in the doorway of his mother's bedroom, he said, "You two can sleep in here." I frowned at him and nodded. After the tour, the three of us stood in the kitchen, looking at what Pablo was cooking on the stove. He was making pumpkin ravioli with a hint of truffle oil and mixing an endive salad, and in a pan on the stove was an oily, garlic-drenched pile of escargot. I told Adrea what it was. She said, "I know they eat snails in France, I was prepared."

Adrea began exploring the place; she examined all the ceramic cats on the kitchen window ledge. She petted each one with a single stroke of her finger. The real cat we'd encountered in his mother's room had made her jump in fright. I leaned my head against Pablo's back while he cooked, feeling needy and clingy, scared of my own feelings.

Pablo continued preparing the meal. He was happy to see us and seemed at ease. "What have you seen? What are your favorite places? Tell me everything."

"The Louvre. I go to the Musée d'Orsay constantly, but it's not my favorite. I like the Rodin museum the most, probably." I sounded boring to myself. I wanted to be light and comfortable with Pablo, but I inexplicably felt like I needed to cry in his arms before I could relax.

Adrea turned around from the window, looking straight at me. It seemed as if she were looking right into me, knowing how unnatural I felt. I winked at her, and she smiled back, touching one eye with her fingertips, making it shut.

I turned to Pablo. "It's great to be here with you." I laughed. "I think I feel shy."

He dropped the wooden spoon on the counter and put his arms around me. "You missed me. Oh, you poor girl, you've been missing me."

I laughed again. "I did." He was tickling my waist. "It's hard to be apart from me," he teased.

"Stop. Okay, I'm over it now." I tried to stop smiling.

"Good, I have to cook and—not in front of the child," he said, pointing at Adrea, teasing me further.

"Very funny. Do you want help?"

"It's ready." He handed me a stack of three plates. "Let's set the table."

After dinner I took Adrea upstairs to get ready for bed. I looked into the guest room where Pablo was sleeping. There was a small twin bed; his shirts were stacked on the chair, shoes and books on the floor. I wondered if he had been writing.

Early the following morning I unpacked our small bag before taking Adrea to the school. Adrea bounced on his mother's high bed while I hung my clothes in the closet. I couldn't help thinking that his mother would be uptight at the sight of us in her bedroom.

After I finished putting my clothes on hangers, I started riffling through her clothes. She was taller than I'd imagined, my height it seemed. Her clothes were stylish and conservative. I heard the springs of the bed bouncing and a new sound. I imagined Adrea patting her hand over her open mouth, like the *wha-wha* imitation of an American Indian. It didn't dawn on me right away that she was making some type of word sound.

I turned around from the closet to see her looking right at me, making the exact gesture I'd imagined, with the muffled sound vibrating from her lips. She was still rocking up and down on the mattress on her knees. She removed her hand from her mouth, pronounced "Mmuh," and as a separate piece, "mee."

I stared. She pointed at me, smiling, and repeated, "Mummy."

My mind leaped back to our first weeks together, the tiredness, the fear and doubt, my heart palpitations. I remembered Adrea at five, standing barefoot over a pile of broken dishes and glass in our kitchen, my first feelings of anger toward her. And what had grown out of that endurance was belonging. It was from that moment on that I desired to hear her call me Mommy. The way Megan and I called for our mother, I wanted to be called.

Two years later, in another mother's house, far from home, I gazed at the lovely girl who was equally devoted to the family unit we'd become. The girl who had gone against nature to name me as her mother and whom fate had conceded to make my child. Something I realized I needed no proof of. Then I rushed to the bed, knocking her over, holding her small body to me, her face hooked over my shoulder, tucked tight.

I took Adrea to school and came straight back to the apartment. Pablo and I drank coffee and spent the rest of the morning in his mother's bed. I did cry, as I'd imagined the night before, but instead of shedding tears of insecurity, I was overwhelmed by gratitude. The luckiness of having Pablo's love again and the reward of hearing Adrea's voice calling me mother filled me.

We lay in bed for a couple hours, not sleeping but resting with our eyes closed, arms around each other.

Eventually I got up and lifted the window open. The air brought goose bumps to my skin. "It's so fresh outside, let's go for a walk and eat."

"Hmm, soon," Pablo mumbled.

I squirmed back in beside him. "Are you feeling nostalgic? We used to stay in bed like this in college."

"Then it was lazy, now it's earned." He pulled my hair forward from my shoulder, brushing my nipple with the ends of it. "Last week when I was staying with my mother in the countryside, I met this old man she knows, a farmer. He had worked for a vineyard and a rose farm when he was younger. His whole life, he'd worked the land, since he was seventeen, providing for his wife and children. And now she's dead and they're all gone, working in frivolous professions like banking and advertising. That's what he told me."

"Sounds like a fable." I pulled the blanket up over my shoulder.

"And he was so happy to meet me, 'the widow's son,' wearing good solid clothes, doesn't even own a suit, who could drink wine with him in the middle of the day. We were talking about good meat, and he thought I was a butcher. More than anything in the world, I wanted to be a butcher that afternoon. I loved the idea of being a butcher."

"What did you tell him?"

"I said, 'Actually, monsieur, I'm a poet by profession.' And it was all wrong, the 'monsieur,' the 'by profession.' He walked away, went inside his house."

"Maybe he needed to go inside and cry for a minute, or go to the bathroom, or jot down some item on his grocery list. Besides, you are a butcher. You should have told him you're a butcher of words." I tried to lighten his mood. "Poetry brings beauty to people; the little prince says that it is because something is beautiful that it is truly useful."

Pablo smiled briefly. "Do you like my poetry?"

I lay back down on my stomach, next to him, lowering

my voice. "Pab, I love your story about the old man and I love your poetry. Let's take a shower and go out, okay?"

"You get the water hot, I'll meet you."

While I stood in the bathroom, leaning against the tile wall outside the shower, I realized I hadn't said I loved him. Why was it hard to say the obvious?

Later that afternoon, alone in a small park, I watched a mother and her baby playing on the swings. I could imagine my own mother pushing Megan on our backyard swing set. I remembered being one of two children stretched out in the tub or splayed together on the bed. My mother once observed me with ownership, entitlement. In the days when my mother felt entitled to possess me, before she was the mother of a dead child.

This was tied in with my feelings about Adrea's speaking. I felt bonded to Katrice and the other teachers for their role in opening this door. I imagined the parents of some of my kids at school, feeling this kind of attraction to me. I thought of the hearing parents, how they sometimes grew dependent. But what they became attached to was the dream of communicating with their child. Something they saw me as capable of doing for them.

I was being pulled back toward the past on this trip. Adrea's changing brought Megan and even my child self lurking in the corners of my mind. The girls that both slipped away. Because that careless confidant girl I was had disappeared in the water as surely as Megan did. And my mother had not surfaced for air even once.

Adrea sat on the floor in a black leotard, her legs spread wide apart. She twisted around toward me, keeping her back perfectly straight. We were going back to our dorm room later that night. I packed our suitcase, absentmindedly watching Adrea lean to the left and then to the right.

Her arms curved above her head. She had wound her curly hair into a bun. She'd had a growth spurt on the trip; her legs looked longer, her body more slender.

I stomped on the floor and signed to her, "You make a good ballerina." She smiled and stood up, lifting her body from her toes. She walked on her toes over to the dresser mirror in Pablo's mother's room, looking at herself with concentration. I watched her watching herself, and the image of the little prince alighting on a new planet came to me.

Adrea turned from the mirror and signed to me, "Do I look Spanish?"

I gazed back at her and nodded. She crossed the room and perched herself on the bed. I continued to watch her, hoping that she would let me in on her thoughts and not flit off to something else. She curled her fingers under her chin for a moment and then flung them out quickly, signing, "Did you ever meet my parents?"

"No." I smiled weakly. When I met you, you were living with Mrs. Carter. Remember?" She nodded. "Have you been thinking about your parents?"

She shifted to tuck one leg beneath her; with her hands low, practically in her lap, she signed, "Did they give me away because I'm deaf?"

I wondered if she was working through the things Xavier had said about his past.

I considered the circumstance of her birth. Her parents holding on to her those long and short months, celebrating her first birthday, they must have, and then giving her away, reshaping themselves into two parts instead of three.

"That may have been one of the reasons. They were young; maybe they didn't have enough money to get things they needed. They probably didn't know anything about deafness." I paused to gauge her reaction.

Adrea ran her hand across her head and tugged at the bun she'd made. I looked at our half-packed suitcase. The room darkened slightly with the departing sun. "Adrea, I never met them. I never tried to find out more about them. I thought maybe one day you would want to, when you're older." I felt rotten speaking this way to her.

She smiled in a pitiful way, like a wall cracking. "If I wasn't deaf I'd be a different girl. I'd be her."

The sign for "her" was only a finger pointing back to all the other signs, the one we've been talking about. It could also mean "there," which I guess was the same thing in this instance. I only stared. Adrea made the sign for a drink of water, hopped off the bed, and walked out of the room. I lay back and breathed deeply, feeling the weight of my body and the bed beneath me. Speaking out loud, where I was alone, I asked, "Who would I be?"

We returned to the dorm for the final week of the program. Katrice met me outside the school at nine in the morning, asking, "Did you eat something yet?" She said we would go back to her house and she would cook for me. Then she wanted to take me around to her favorite shops. She had the day off from school and had offered to take me around Paris, like friends, I thought.

We got into her red miniature box of a car, and the radio came on loud to a heated discussion on a talk show. Although I was now practically fluent in French sign, I didn't know the spoken language at all. I'd experienced a sort of deafness of my own. Stopped at an intersection, Katrice turned toward me, her knees actually bumping into mine. "We have a drive, twenty-five minutes or so," she said, taking off with the light, riding very close to the car in front of us. I had always been a pedestrian in Paris, rarely being part of the herd of dense traffic. We left the city limits, and saw a part of the suburbs that was completely new to me. The winding hilly roads made me think of an island village. We took a series of uphill turns, Katrice calling out historical street names and interesting sights to me. I caught glimpses of well-tended gardens, each house unique.

Our flower garden in the backyard of our house in Boston loomed up in my mind. I saw Megan crouching in the grass, holding a baby bird with a broken neck in her cupped hands, grieving over the lost life. I closed my eyes on the memory. The car stopped short, and Katrice was already getting out. I felt old.

We entered the front yard through a low gate, which Katrice latched closed behind us. She had a manicured garden with an ornate birdbath. In front of her door she stopped abruptly. "You don't mind dogs, do you?"

I shook my head. "I like dogs." As she turned the key, I heard an excited whine just inside the door, and then it swung inward on a handsome Great Dane. He shimmied backward with pleasure, and Katrice spoke to him in English, "Surprised to see me this soon? You happy fool." He rushed past us and ran laps around the small yard. Katrice said, "That's Gustav." She called him and he came loping back, squeezing in through the closing door.

We entered a dimly lit room. Katrice walked straight through to the kitchen at the other end of the house. Gustav was on her heels, and I followed him. Katrice examined the inside of her refrigerator and started pulling out breakfast items. She looked down at her arms full of items and seemed to hesitate before speaking. "Forgive me, coffee first, let me fix you an espresso." I smiled at the natural pleasure of speaking with your hands full, of being with a new friend. I leaned against the counter and carefully gazed around the room. I thought: let me be as observant as Adrea.

Katrice said, "While I cook, look around, feel comfortable."

As I walked back into the living room, Gustav laboriously got up off the kitchen floor and trotted after me. He poked his nose into my palm, mildly wagging his tail. "Okay, fellow, you keep an eye on me."

The historic-looking room made me think of inheritance. Two walls were lined with bookshelves. The books looked like antiques, French and German. I scanned them briefly for anything in English, feeling ignorant in my one plain language. I instinctively signed, "No, I'm bilingual, right Gustav?" He licked my extended fingers, and I repeated in French sign, "I know several languages, you big dog." I wiped my fingers on top of his soft head. I studied a cluster of framed snapshots on an end table. Gustav settled heavily beside me, his chin resting on my foot.

It had to be her mother. Her hair was darker than Katrice's and fell heavily around her shoulders. Her mouth was open, relinquishing a smile, giving in to the photographer, whom I guessed was her husband. She looked intelligent. There was playfulness around the corners of her mouth, which had made its way into Katrice. I wondered if she was still living and nearby.

I tried to imagine a photograph of my mother like this one. If her character could be captured, what would someone see? The distance between my mother and me felt immense, actually as though she were no longer living. I told Gustav, "There is an ocean between us. That's a pun." His look told me he knew it wasn't funny. The separation I felt was not new or temporary or about geography. My legs were aching from squatting there, and I slumped down onto the floor. Looking at my long legs covered by thin black stockings, I thought, I am the woman like her that I had once hoped to become. I am an adult, a mother, and I have her to thank for it. I turned to see Katrice framed in the sunlit doorway.

She came over and held out her hands, pulling me up from my place on the floor. "I see Adrea in you."

"Nobody has before."

"Maybe here, apart from everything you know, you merge more. Is that how you say it, come together?"

I nodded, pulling my hair forward across my face, like protection. I pictured Adrea and me sleeping in our dorm room bed, her narrow backside pushed into my stomach. I thought back on our history. Love, we always had, but we had come to find ease lately too. It would feel strange to go home and sleep in our separate rooms.

I sat at the kitchen table. Katrice laid out toast and butter, the espresso, orange juice. Gustav settled down again under the kitchen table. There was a rounded pitcher on the table full of flowers from the garden. Some petals had dropped and lay around the place settings. I rolled a velvety petal beneath my fingertip.

Katrice brought over two large plates of eggs and sat down across from me. "My mother was raised in the old-school philosophy that the deaf should learn how to speak, no signing. After she got herself released from the mental hospital, a well-meaning woman from the social service got her enrolled in a residential school for the deaf." Katrice paused to take several bites of her eggs. I thought of the intense face in the photo, and I remembered what Xavier had said about Katrice's mother. I was nervous about what Katrice might reveal. "The school demanded that all the students speak; after all, there's nothing wrong with their voices, only their ears." Her voice contained a bitter edge. "She was so smart, she knew they wanted her to repeat the words they were saying, and she would try, but it was meaningless to her. She really didn't understand anything."

I had almost finished my entire breakfast, and Katrice had hardly touched hers. I was eating too fast and my stomach felt queasy. I said, "She must have been incredibly lonely."

"Each time she repeated a word incorrectly they would dunk her head in a bucket of water, longer each time."

Katrice massaged her forehead, frowning. "After a few dunkings she could not speak at all."

"She was nearly drowned for being deaf," I said numbly. I didn't want to make the connection. I didn't want to form an image of this in my mind.

"It was the norm then, as though it were a deviant behavior to be deaf." Katrice focused her attention on her plate and ate quickly now. She cleared our dishes to the sink and looked at me intently. The room felt too warm.

Katrice sat again, oblivious to my discomfort. "My mom reads lips and speaks now; she isn't even fluent in sign. My father was hearing, he never learned sign language." Katrice seemed to slowly come back to the present moment, remembering I was in the room.

I felt listless from the food, the heat, her story. My arms lay on the table like two inert objects. She touched the inside of one arm, where I saw a course of blue veins.

Her touch made my breath catch, making a thin scrap of sound that embarrassed me. Katrice put her hand up to my forehead. "Are you all right?"

I closed my eyes. Katrice's fingers gently held my head. I leaned into her hand, and tears seeped out mercilessly.

I saw Megan in my mind, rushing backward, receding. Stay, I wanted to yell, but she couldn't. Up close I saw her eyes. Her whispers, like hot cinnamon. She would tell me things, husky and flirtatious, she would tell me everything, except that she was going, except good-bye.

I felt Katrice remove her hands. I was embarrassed by my emotions, but my mind receded further. I saw my mother dropping the camera, racing to the water. I saw her coming home to my father and me, suitcase in hand, and turned away in a photograph, unable to look at me. She'd lost Megan due to pride or too much self-assurance, such certainty of self, a mother's mistake. Do not look at her sister, she thinks. Do not turn her into salt with your stare.

Katrice was standing bent over my chair, her arms around my shoulders.

I was still there though. You were still my mother. I thought you knew everything. I thought we were always protected. I loved seeing you carry her. I helped feed her. I taught her to swim. We were fish together. Little girls, sisters, are fish together. I was the big fish, and that's why I swam away too soon. But you were a fish too, Mother. But you let go, and maybe, I let go too.

I opened my eyes. Katrice handed me a used napkin from the table and I wiped my nose. I laughed. "Sorry." Katrice tugged my hair, an affectionate gesture I'd seen her do to Adrea. She settled back in her chair.

I thought of Adrea, squatting on sturdy feet in the Hearing Center's garden. Her head of curls lifted, with bright hands speaking, the sweetest child.

"You okay?"

I blew my nose, smiled at her, I was okay. "You know Adrea's adopted?"

"Yes," Katrice said quietly.

"I deeply wanted Adrea, but I've always been afraid that I'm not a good enough mother. I had a sister who drowned. I've been afraid that Adrea was a replacement for her. I've never said that out loud before."

Katrice shook her head firmly. "No," she said to the room, not a response to me, just generally not accepting what I had said. "You feel insecure. Maybe you did want a little girl because of your sister, but that doesn't matter, you have a real daughter now and Adrea has a mommy now."

> The birds sing, sing, sing, but I hear them not at all,
> darn, darn, darn
> The cats meow, meow, meow, but I hear the
>   not at all
> darn, darn, darn

The cows moo, moo, moo, but I hear them not
　　at all,
darn, darn, darn.

I hung in the open doorway watching, shocked by this deaf children's song. Adrea saw me and smiled, and they started up again. It took me a moment to realize that they were signing, not singing. The room was filled with the rhythm of the song. The teacher stood by the board; arm swinging, she playfully pointed to Birds—Sing; Cats—Meow; Cows—Moo, where the phrases were written down.

All the children, on the verge of laughter, signed, "but I hear them not at all," and then ferociously, with joy, they dipped one hand, snapping their fingers, "darn," and then twice more, "darn, darn." They were perfectly synchronized, and the room resounded with the song.

It was incredibly beautiful. I preserved the entire moment, the room, the children, the rhythmic snapping, in my mind. I thought to share this plain happiness with Pablo and Bonnie, like his poems or her feeling a baby's kick from inside, something just right. I wished my parents could see too, what isn't lost, what you always still have left.

Adrea ran up, beaming; she slapped her hands on my thighs. I reached down and stroked her little face, kissed her fingers before she pulled them away. "I learned a song!" her hands shouted.

"I heard it," I said.

Gripping my hands, Adrea leaned back on her heels, her head falling back, her glistening eyes resting on me; she smiled peacefully.

After school Katrice drove us the half mile home to the dormitory. Adrea sat in the backseat, still singing with her hands. I listened to the three snaps of "darn," like messengers.

"You don't know it?" Katrice said.

"The song? No, I've never heard it before."

"It's American. I think it was popular there at some time. I don't know its origin. There are several ASL songs with the one-two, one-two-three rhythm. They are sung in groups, to incite a sense of togetherness."

"Adrea seems to like it all by herself." I gestured toward my oblivious, happy daughter.

We played together on the floor before bedtime. Passing her doll back and forth, I planted a kiss on the doll's lips, then pressed its face into Adrea's neck, tickling her. I signed, "I think I'm almost ready to go home."

"Me too," she said easily. "You want me to teach you 'darn, darn, darn'?"

"Yes, please."

We repeated the song five or six times until we were in perfect harmony. Adrea's face took on the same thrilled expression she'd had in the classroom. I thought, she likes to sing as much as I do. As we finished the chorus, I signed, "A song in my heart."

Adrea raised up on her knees excitedly, answering, "Food in my belly."

We finished together, "And love in my family."

Katrice and I sat on the low wall of a fountain in the Jardin du Luxembourg, watching a small group of children racing their toy boats in the water. These well-crafted vessels had thin wooden poles that the child held on to, securing and guiding the boat. There were swans in the pond too, such fairy-tale creatures. I thought about ugly ducklings becoming swans. I thought of the children at the Hearing Center, whom I felt a sudden pang for, each of them ducklings and swans.

Adrea and Pablo were heading back toward us from their apparently successful quest to find an ice-cream cart.

Katrice said, "They seem very close."

I felt self-conscious. I wasn't sure how to describe him. "He's a big part of my life."

Pablo and Adrea stopped at the pond to watch the boats. He kneeled down beside her, pointing at the different models, catching the drips from the side of his ice cream in his mouth. Adrea held hers in one hand, forgotten, while she stared at the other children. She started signing PRETTY and BEAUTIFUL. I watched part of her ice cream fall off into the grass. Adrea noticed too, returning her attention to licking the remains.

Pablo and Adrea began walking back. When they reached us Katrice made a joke to Pablo in French. Adrea stood on the edge of the fountain we'd been sitting on. I listened to Pablo and Katrice's soft banter for a moment. I saw Pablo through her eyes, his physical beauty, gentleness, and attentiveness to others, and I felt fortunate again for having him back in my life. I motioned to Adrea to climb on my back, and I walked down the hill to the pond with her. She wanted to show me the swans.

The next day I met Pablo for a farewell lunch. Our trip would be over in a matter of days; he would be staying a while longer, he wasn't sure how long. We ate crepes at a sidewalk café. Pablo told me a story about his childhood in Paris. "My mother had left me in a playground outside a doctor's office while she went in for an appointment. The playground was surrounded by a high fence, there were many children and mothers and fathers inside. She left me for an hour and told me where she was going and to not leave the fenced area."

"How old were you? Were you scared?"

Pablo wiped his mouth with his napkin. "I remember very clearly feeling alone in the city, forgetting where my mother was or why I was by myself sitting on a swing. It was a strange surprise when she returned, wobbling on her heels in the sand. I saw her as a stranger would."

I swallowed my food. "You didn't recognize her, or you saw her through others' eyes?"

Pablo smiled shyly. "It was the first time I felt aware of her appearance, a physical awareness of her." He blushed. "I saw that she was attractive. I was embarrassed; I walked home keeping my distance from her on the sidewalk."

I could see that young Pablo inside the man in front of me. I grabbed one of his hands and kissed it. He had turned out all right. His hand still clutched in mine, it was possible to have hope that we all could.

With only three days left in France, I was very excited by Katrice's invitation to have lunch with her and her mother. As soon as Katrice proposed that we meet, I began comparing the person whom I imagined Katrice's mother to be to my own mother. I prepared myself to meet a woman who was whole and present. I imagined how Katrice must cherish her mother and enjoy spending time with her. I thought her mother would embody everything I desired in a maternal figure, everything I longed to be for Adrea.

I took the hour-long bus ride out to Katrice's house. When I approached the front of the house I slowed my gait, wanting to check myself before entering the yard. Before I stepped into view I saw them, seated at an iron table in the yard. Katrice faced me, her head tilted to the side, resting in her own hand, watching her mother, listening. I saw her mother's back, her hair long and dark, her shoulders wrapped in a red shawl. Her hands were not moving. Katrice gazed directly at her mother, with a tired expression on her face; she too was not speaking. I felt I was witnessing an intimate moment, a meaningful silence.

I stepped up to the gate and waved to Katrice. Her head sprung up from its resting place in her palm and her face lit up. They rose from the table as I approached, and both kissed each side of my face. Katrice signed, "This is my mother." Her mother put forth her hand to clasp mine, a gesture that never starts a conversation among the Deaf. Usually names are spelled out for one another, or you show your name sign, say pleased to meet you, and then people shake hands.

With my hand held loosely in her own, Katrice's mother spoke to me in French. "It is a pleasure to meet you, Anna. Please call me Martine." She smiled in a very poised manner. Katrice promptly translated. I didn't know how to respond. I already knew from Katrice that her mother preferred speech to sign. Yet she was completely deaf. It seemed rude to only speak to a deaf person even if the person knew how to lip-read. For the first time in my life, I felt as though I were meeting someone who was "passing," that Katrice's mother actually desired to be perceived as hearing. I spoke and signed, "I have been looking forward to meeting you," keeping my signing casual, my hands barely forming the shapes.

She turned to Katrice, saying something in French. Katrice looked at me, her eyes somewhat flat. She asked, "Would you like something to drink?"

"Sure," I said, my voice booming out too loud. Katrice smiled in an embarrassed way, turning to go into the house. Her mother gestured toward the chairs. "*S'il vous plaît*, sit." I sat and smiled at her, looking past her shoulder to the thick tree out on the sidewalk that I had stood behind and observed them from. Martine had been talking to Katrice. Katrice had been listening; her deaf mother had been talking to her because she prefers to talk.

The three of us stood in the kitchen together, each working at preparing part of the lunch, each with a wineglass resting nearby. I made Maritza's salad dressing, lime juice and oil, with lots of crushed garlic. Gustav rotated his large slate head to keep any eye on all three of us; I felt very connected to his simple dogness.

Martine continued to speak to her daughter in French. Katrice responded in French as well and translated into English for me. I would have preferred to cook in silence and drift off while they talked. It was awkward and disheartening. We did not have a language in common, French sign being the closest—and Martine was not fluent. But Martine preferred to speak and have Katrice translate, everything occurring through speech, not allowing for deafness. The afternoon passed for me in quiet sadness.

After lunch I walked down Katrice's suburban street to the bus stop, where I'd catch an express bus back to the Paris city center. I thought of how we all carry forward the weight of our life's history and that of our parents.

During Adrea's last days of school, my trip moved toward its end the same way it had begun, in solitude. Pablo was traveling with his mother. I wandered around the outlying suburbs of Paris, through areas I hadn't visited before. I found where the houses ran together in dilapidated rows, where children ran about in the street dressed in thin cotton pants and leather shoes, riding bicycles in mad race games. The women, all immigrants, stood on stoops, in long cotton skirts, scarves or kerchiefs tied on their heads. They leaned and talked with each other, and the children ran about yelling in shrieking voices; this was Parisian poverty. I walked through these streets at dusk and was conspicuous as a tourist where tourists don't venture. Although I was watched from one end of the block to the other, it was not with hostility. I suppose I watched back. I never felt alone on those walks.

I walked through our last night in Paris too. After I tucked Adrea in bed, I asked the woman next-door in the dorm to watch out for her, and I went out. I found other new areas. The night was wet, a mist turning into a light rain. The black paved streets turned shiny and reflective, my hair held tiny crystals of water. One street was lit up with street lamps; its storefronts dark tinted glass. Occasionally doors swung open to let out harsh music and voices like exhaust. They were nightclubs for Paris's youth. Just like urban girls anywhere, wearing fishnet stockings and ratty fur coats, they could be young women from London or the East Village. They smoked cigarettes and were shrill and beautiful. I smiled to myself watching these teenage girls. Their destinies lay ahead undiscovered. Adrea has all the same mystery to unfold for herself that these tough independent girls do. I felt a new confidence in her making her own way in the world, in her strength. Nothing needed fixing, only everyday tending to. Returning to the dorm, I was astounded to see it was already early morning. Adrea would shake me awake just a few hours later.

Conducting all of our good-byes on the last day of school had been exhausting. And saying good-bye to Katrice was especially difficult for me and for Adrea, but I knew we'd stay in touch, and Katrice promised to visit us in New York. Finally I had begun to feel restless to embark on our long flight and to be alone in my own city.

Our return flight was a contrast to the flight over. This time Adrea slept almost the whole way and ate quietly when I woke her up for dinner. I slept too, or just rested with my eyes closed. When Adrea fell back to sleep, I drew in her coloring book, enjoying the thoughtless filling in of shapes with color.

Back at home, Adrea and I had a weekend of readjusting before returning to the Hearing Center. We woke up very late, and I cooked brunch. She watched television while I ran up and down with load after load of our laundry. We fell asleep together on the couch. Later, we ordered our favorite Chinese food, which we hadn't eaten in six weeks. We both took baths and went to bed early. Adrea kicked around in her own bed, enjoying the feel of new sheets to herself. I said good night only once; she needed no urging to sleep.

The next day we still had jet lag. Adrea said, "My body doesn't know if it's morning or night." I had some anxiety about returning to the Center, already anticipating the catching up. Later that night I set the alarm and reminded Adrea that we would go to the Center the next day. Then I couldn't sleep. I opened a bottle of wine and decided to call my parents. When I heard my father's greeting on the answering machine, I hung up. I called a second time and quickly stated that we were home safe. I knew it would be my father who'd call back.

I wished Pablo were in New York. It was too late to call Bonnie. I thought of calling Maritza on the TTY, but I knew she would ask about Adrea, and I didn't want to preface their reunion with anything. Maritza would see the subtle changes in Adrea more than I could describe anyway.

Looking in my closets and desk, I marveled at the huge amount of possessions. After spending six weeks living with only necessities, there was a frivolity to my belongings. I began to clean out the drawers of my desk. Then I filled an entire garbage bag with objects I'd been holding on to: hats, junk jewelry, unworn sweaters, paper weights and old foreign coins, trinkets from other people's trips. I felt I could get rid of almost everything and that my home itself was losing unnecessary weight.

In the back of a desk drawer, I wrapped my hand around a square object and pried it out. There in my hands sat Megan's music box. Its white surface yellowed with age, buried away and forgotten. I turned it around and around. I could remember the last time I sat in her tiny bedroom holding this same music box, Megan dead, all of her things made useless. My hands trembled. I was scared to open it and see if it still made music. I turned the metal winder and opened the box. A plastic ballerina turned, the music twinkled.

I took out a sheet of blank paper and began a letter to my mother. I told her about the trip, what Adrea did in school, I described the classroom and mentioned Katrice. I told her how I was drawn to Katrice, what a wonderful teacher she was. I told her I spent time with Pablo in Paris. I described the African immigrant neighborhoods, which I knew she would have visited too. I said we were happy to be home and tired. I asked her to come visit. "Maybe it's time for you to make another visit? Adrea's grown so much, it would be nice for you to see her, for us to see each other."

My dream began the same as it had on our first night in France. I was in an old room, heavy beams holding it up, like a stable. I could see an old man from the back, wearing a black cap on his head. When he turned around I saw a bulky canvas sack in his arms. I remembered the dead foal before I saw it. He walked toward me, smiling, and turned back a flap of the bag. I saw the small horse's head, red fur wet with sweat. I knew it was only newly dead. The man's face was familiar and kind, with a bristly growth of stubble. This time the dream went further. He spoke to me with a French accent. His words had a golden quality; they came forth from him like bursts of muted light. "It is hearing." He rocked the dead animal lovingly in his arms. He smiled sympathetically toward me. I touched the foal's face and cupped its small muzzle in my hand. The old man tilted his head from the horse to me. He said, "It's all right now, we'll bury it."

We rode the subway down to the Hearing Center. When one seat opened up, Adrea refused to take it. I sat in front of her while she swayed against the pole, looking about bemusedly. She was wearing a skirt we had not taken to France, a plaid kilt with a big silver pin on the side. I was sure the skirt was higher above her knees than before.

Arriving first, we unlocked the Center door. Adrea ran in and looked around. I put my bags and coat on a desk and signed to Adrea, "Get your coat off the floor." She threw it on the table and started trying out some new puzzles from the bookshelf. I walked around, spotting all the new things. We were constantly receiving donations, some of which we turned around and donated elsewhere. Our inventory of books and toys, school supplies, even furniture, was continually renewed. I examined the monthly calendar on the wall, observing what Maritza had done per usual and what innovations she'd made in my absence. Two students arrived, and while I caught up with their mothers, I watched Adrea with her classmates. There was a tender shyness that reminded me of Bambi and his doe friend, displaying new antlers and nimble limbs. Adrea placed her hands on her hips while she stood back, listening to her friends' stories of what she had missed. Then she described odd details of her trip, things I hadn't made my own impressions from. She told them that there were no desks in the school, that they ate breakfast at ten thirty instead of lunch, and how the billboards had nudes on them. I noticed that her signing was more eloquent. She moved her fingers more deliberately with sharpness. She'd painted her small fingernails red.

Everyone seemed to arrive at the same time. Maritza was there, kneeling on the floor next to Adrea, her hands clasping one knee, watching Adrea's rapid signing with a look of pure pleasure on her face. I was, as always, eager to observe the way Maritza loves Adrea. Adrea made a move to show Maritza some of the ballet performance we'd seen our last week in Paris. Maritza stood up and stepped back to give her room, and Adrea's foot accidentally kicked Maritza's lunch bag across the floor. Adrea stuck her neck out, making her jaw jut forward, and said the single word "Sorry." Maritza immediately caught the oral movement, and being a lip-reader, knew the meaning as well. When Maritza stared, Adrea brought her closed hand to her chest and made the sign for "sorry." Maritza touched the top of Adrea's head and smiled gently at her. I held my hand half raised to greet Maritza. I was strangely hoping that Maritza would know that Adrea was not speaking much, that she had begun learning to lip-read and could pronounce an occasional word. I wanted her to know that I was satisfied—more, that I only desired Adrea to be a strong deaf person.

Maritza looked at me, a smile slowly emerging. We stepped forward to embrace.

One of Adrea's new interests since our trip was watching the Discovery channel in closed captions. If I was in the kitchen or bedroom, she'd come running in to fingerspell a word she saw in closed captions that she didn't know the meaning of. When I showed her the sign, she always looked exasperated because she knew the word, it was just the English she wasn't familiar with. I was always amazed how, even with the long difficult words, she remembered the exact spelling.

Adrea came running into my room. Lightly slapping the backs of my thighs for attention, she asked, "What is H-A-N-D-I-C-A-P-P-E-D?" I drew a blank. I couldn't think of a sign for "handicapped." I said, "It might mean people who have problems with their bodies, like people who use wheelchairs." Adrea gave me the look she has when she thinks I've given a poor explanation, and she ran back out of the room. I returned to putting clean sheets on the bed. It occurred to me that she could be watching something about deafness. I went to see.

There was a white woman holding a black baby. Without

reading the captions, I couldn't tell if either mother or child was handicapped and I wondered if it had anything to do with adoption. I sat down on the couch behind where Adrea was sitting on the floor. I tapped her on the shoulder and motioned for her to move back: "Not so close, your eyes." I turned the sound on. The woman was saying that she and her husband had gone to classes to learn how to take care of a baby. Before they got married they were instructed on how to keep an apartment, go grocery shopping, do housework, use public transportation. The camera turned so her husband was in the picture. He was black and she was white. They were both developmentally disabled. The program began discussing the school they attended and the legal battle they'd gone through to gain the right to marry and have a child. They showed another married couple who'd also had a baby after finishing the required courses. I was baffled as to the state's role in these people's lives. The two women were talking with each other about what they went through gaining their freedom. The first woman said, "Other women can have a baby without even thinking about it, not knowing anything about babies, but I have to go to classes and practice." The second woman, ignoring her comment, said, "But why is your husband black and you're white and your baby's tan?" Adrea didn't make a peep. I doubted this made any sense to her at all. The woman responded, "Maybe because I like it that way." I laughed out loud.

Adrea lay down on the rug, resting her head in her hands. She didn't have any questions. I went to start dinner.

The volume was still on, and I listened from the kitchen as I washed the lettuce one leaf at a time. The word "handicapped" played again and again in my mind. If Adrea ever attended a mainstream public school or went to a hearing college, she would probably be the only deaf person in her class, she would be the handicapped girl. I tried to remember exactly how I defined the word to her half an hour ago, something about abilities. I put the lettuce in the spinner and carried it into the living room. I sat back on the couch and handed the spinner to Adrea. She shut off the TV and, gripping the bowl against her stomach, cranked the knob. Her body rocked with the force. I stomped my foot on the floor and she looked up from her labor, her hand automatically slowing down.

"Do you understand what handicapped means?" She set the spinner by her feet. "Yes, I know that word from Mrs. Carter, I forgot."

"What did Mrs. Carter say about it?"

"She said she had a house for handicapped children, that was her job."

"For deaf children," I corrected. "Being deaf can be considered a handicap. What do you think of that?"

"It's O-K. Why were those women on TV handicapped?"

"They were slow, something in their brains works more slowly. It's harder for them to think quickly and clearly all the time; they were mentally handicapped."

She looked down and put her foot on top of the spinner, wobbling slightly on her other foot. "Will I be able to have a baby?"

I grabbed her small hand and kissed the back of it. "Yes, you can have children and get married and have a job and do anything you want to do."

"I know, but can I have a baby in my belly?"

"Yes, when you're a woman you'll be able to make a baby in your belly."

"Are you handicapped too?"

I leaned back into the couch. If this whole, wise child was considered handicapped, then shouldn't I be?

"No, not that I know of."

"Why couldn't you make a baby?"

I smiled in surprise. "I could, I wanted you to be my baby. I chose you." I poked her stomach.

She picked up the spinner and gave it a few good turns, then stopped. She examined my face, her eyes squinting, lashes crossing top over bottom. "Mrs. Carter said that people who couldn't have children would adopt us."

"She was wrong." I repeated the sign WRONG to Adrea, shaking my head to go with it. Maybe I had thought that too, unable or not allowed. "No, that's not true for me, for us. You were exactly what I wanted, my first choice. Okay?"

O-K.

I opened my arms, but instead of a hug she sat in my lap and began spinning the lettuce some more. I squeezed her until she uttered, with the sound of a weight on her tongue, "Stop."

I let her go. "Adrea, you know if you work hard you can go to college, to Gallaudet or any college and you can do any kind of job you want when you grow up. Deaf people can do everything that hearing people can do."

"Okay, Mom," she signed, "what's for dinner?"

I pulled a long imaginary strand of spaghetti out of my mouth and she bit the end of it from my fingers.

There is a 180-degree space around a deaf person, a half circle. This space is constantly used in signing. There are forty-three hand shapes, yet there are thousands of signs. Much depends on the way the palm faces. There is irony; signing makes beautiful noises, hands rubbing together, clapping, knuckles knocking. There is deaf and Deaf. Lowercase *deaf* describes the condition of not hearing, while *Deaf* refers to the culture, the culture inseparable from sign.

The Hearing Center's students range from hard of hearing to completely deaf. There is a bit of segregation, not in the activities we do, but many of the hard of hearing kids have speech therapists, take dance classes; it is undoubtedly a very different experience from being deaf. At the Hearing Center, sign language is the primary mode of communication, yet I notice that most of the hard of hearing kids stick together. During lunch there will be a table that would appear like any other group of school children having lunch. They are verbal. They speak to each other, they shout like any kids, their hands hold sandwiches, cups of applesauce, are busy, and they talk. Without hearing the heavy, distorted sounds of their speech and if their hearing aids were hidden, they do not appear deaf.

The other children, including Adrea, who are completely deaf do not take any notice of their verbal classmates, who depart from sign language together only at this time. Other tables are silent, eat slowly, constantly putting down their food to use their hands to speak. They sign constantly, their mouths only moving in expression or eating.

Before I adopted Adrea I observed admiringly the way she would move around the room of children, friends with everyone, never having a single best friend whom she spent all of her time with. When the hard of hearing children made their band with their own lunchtime regime, Adrea never joined them. It was hard to ignore the fact that these hard of hearing, verbal children would have an easier time in the hearing world than the signing deaf children. But what they would lose was the comfort, camaraderie, and totality of a Deaf community and culture.

A few weeks after our return, Adrea was showing two girls at the Center her workbook from Paris. Placing the book down on the table, she explained the instructions, then picked it back up again to show them up close the incomplete sentences she had to fill in. The girls shook their heads from side to side, acknowledging the demands of her assignment. She held the book open under their noses and said, "Haard." I smiled at what sounded like a Boston accent. Adrea was stepping forth into something new, like a skater at a frozen-solid lake, more secure than she knew in her tentative movements.

At the end of the summer, in response to my letter and invitation, my mother came to see us. She arrived late at night. I'd already eaten dinner with Adrea and put her to bed. My mother would be taking a cab directly from the airport, staying at my place for three nights. I paced the apartment waiting for her, dusting and watering plants to pass the time. Once she'd arrived and taken a shower, we sat in the living room to talk. Within an hour, we had exhausted small talk and my mother grew contemplative.

I'd offered her a drink several times before she accepted a glass of orange juice. Now she stared at the full glass on the coffee table before her. "The first time I saw you with Adrea, I noticed." My mother picked up her glass of orange juice, took a purposeful sip; she pressed her lips together. I saw that she was trying to hold herself together, that something was leaking. She placed the glass back on the table after wiping the bottom with her hand.

"We were here in your living room and you were sitting on the floor beneath the window. Your legs were bare, and you stretched them out in front of you in a patch of sunlight on the floor. You were just yourself, and I was feeling so self-conscious." She stopped speaking and smiled at me shyly. I smiled back without really knowing what she was feeling.

That was the last time she had come, the only other time she'd met Adrea. I tried to be patient; it would take all of the three-day visit to get comfortable together.

"You were on the floor, pointing your feet, enjoying the warmth, and I confess I felt distant from you, prim in my chair. I asked you about your work, and I felt as though I were interviewing you. I admired you."

This time we were not on the floor or in the chair, we sat side by side on my couch, and the sky outside my living room window was black. It was night and she'd asked for orange juice and she had things she needed to say, as did I. We needed to address our estrangement. I didn't know where we would begin; one does not apologize for a lifetime, if I was looking for an apology or an explanation. Surely I had not waited all these years for a compliment.

"Adrea must have just woken up from a nap; she walked into the room, groggy, half asleep. She wore jean overalls and no shirt underneath, her hair flung about in every direction. She came and lay her body down along your legs, her head nestled in your lap, and you petted her head and face. Not a sound was exchanged. She fell back asleep, and you all the while kept your eyes on her, listening to my polite talk that meant nothing. You didn't need me to be more, because you had everything you needed right there, contained in a patch of sunlight on the floor."

"I don't know," I said, her memories making me feel despondent.

"Anna, I recognized you. I thought, 'There's Anna—thank God—here is Anna,' and I looked at Adrea too, thinking 'Here is Anna.' I wished I was the mother with a child, wished I was on the floor—a child connected to me, and the realization that you were my child, and that I could touch you, be connected to you, that seemed impossible."

My mother leaned back on the couch, awkwardly pulling at the open collar of her shirt. The top button popped off, racing along the table before it fell on the floor. She said "Oh," laying her hand across her throat. Then she grimaced as though she would cry. I reached for the button. "I was your mother once," she said.

Adrea was very polite to my mother. She did not, in the three days my mother was visiting, draw attention to herself. And she did not pronounce any words in my mother's presence, a resistance I thought I understood.

The next morning when my mother woke up in our house, we all stood in the kitchen. Adrea was cutting herself an apple. She signed to my mother, "Do you want some?" My mother drew her eyebrows together, never understanding the simplest signs. Adrea signed APPLE and lipped the two syllables with it, no sound accompanying. My mother said no, smiling gently, and then said, "Oh," recognizing the change. Adrea brought her plate of apple slices to the table, pulling out a chair, then changing her mind, signed, "I'm going to go draw."

My mother stirred her tea around and around with the spoon as if she would stir it to evaporation. Each sip she took looked awkward, as if the cup didn't suit her mouth. I studied her face. She was still beautiful to me, with long dark hair and large brown eyes. But her face had fallen more since the last time I saw her. When she tilted her head down, I saw a new squareness in her cheeks; they had become weighted and appeared pinned to her cheekbones. She looked sad. I imagined she was happier at a distance from me. She was forcing herself to sit in my kitchen, on the wrong side of the country.

"It's nice that you came, Mom."

"Yes." She smiled feebly. "You asked me to."

I paused. "I wish you wouldn't put it that way."

"What way? I'm glad you wrote and asked me to come."

"Yeah, I know," I sighed. "It just sounds like you felt some obligation to visit us."

"Well, for my sake too. That's a fine reason, Anna, to come see your daughter because it's been too long."

"Yes, it's fine."

My mother had started therapy when she came back to live with my father and me. She saw a psychiatrist for at least a year after Megan's death; she was prescribed Valium. She was prone to generic statements back then, such as the one she'd just made, "That's a fine reason," "People are all unique," "I can imagine how you are feeling."

My mother blinked her eyes, opening them wide, her forehead creasing, preparing to tackle something. "You said in your letter that too much time had been allowed to pass. I don't get the impression now that you were talking about Adrea."

"Adrea's fine. I'm fine too."

She lifted the tea bag out of the cup and, without squeezing it, laid it on the saucer. Her tea was black as coffee. "I'm not. I've been depressed, and I was terrible then, when you were growing up." She looked into her cup with dread and painfully took a sip. I waited. I couldn't draw it out of her, whatever it was. The conversation froze me up. "We talked about having another baby. After just a few months your father said it. I said it too." She wiped at her tears before they even appeared. "But I told your father it was wrong, that you couldn't replace them, not like that, no way. But I was faking some righteous high ground. I lied to him for a year. Said it wasn't right, how could we, that you wouldn't like another sibling. But that wasn't true; I would have done it. I thought it would have saved me to have another child." Her eyes bulged toward me as though I had been the one to say something surprising.

She had another child, and she didn't have the strength to pull herself together for me. "Mom, I don't think you could have handled another child, you weren't functioning well; you couldn't take care of anything." She hadn't been there and I wanted her to finally realize how truly abandoned I was.

She looked at my expressionless face. I could feel her reading it as dismissal, but I wasn't ready to forgive her. "I couldn't take care of you, I know." Tears ran down her cheeks.

I was grateful that Adrea wasn't in the room and couldn't see her mother and grandmother in so much grief, with so little to offer each other. I got my mother a tissue. I put my arms around her shoulders.

"I suppose it's a good thing that I couldn't conceive again."

"You were trying to conceive?" She was only in her thirties, was she my age?

She wiped her eyes with the tissue and laughed lightly at herself. "I guess I was inhospitable." It struck me that we'd moved on without each other. The sum total of the years was both of us lonely and learning not to need each other. The dumb waste of it.

"You know, if Adrea ever stopped needing me, as a confidante, for guidance, as her mother, I think my life would be over. I need her as the only purpose worth a constant effort. Do you know what I mean? Look what's happened to us," I implored, my eyes filling with tears.

She sort of laughed, like a gull skirting away from the waves. "They do stop needing you Anna, but you never stop needing them."

On my mother's last night in New York, we stayed home playing Scrabble. At nine o'clock I told Adrea to kiss her grandma good night and get ready for bed. They hugged, and Adrea went down the hall to brush her teeth and put on pajamas. I felt a rush of sympathy for my mom as I watched the pained expression on her face when she hugged Adrea. We tucked Adrea into bed together, and my mother kissed her again with a sad finality.

We sat in the living room, each reading. I asked her if she wanted wine or tea. I told her I was going to go down to the basement to do some laundry. "Do you want help, or should someone stay in here with Adrea?"

"It would be good for you to stay with Adrea." I sponta-
neously kissed her cheek before going out the door. She
clutched my head briefly.

I stood outside my own front door with the laundry bas-
ket of clean clothes in my hands. I leaned on the door and
listened to the music coming from inside. I knew exactly
the curve of my mother's back, the tilt of her neck, and the
snaking motions of her elbows as she sat at the piano. The
music was simultaneously soothing and sad. She played as
though the piano were an extension of herself, like her own
voice or a replacement for it. I recognized the music but
couldn't place it. It was an old familiar song.

I knew how she felt from just listening outside my apartment. The music had the kind of sadness that is used to
being sad, not even objecting to its own pain. The way I
think of people who have lived many years in war, or a
woman with hungry children.

From beneath the door I saw the light in the hall flick on
and I heard Adrea's sleepy feet dragging along the floor. I
stood up straight, ready to walk in. The piano stopped, and
my mother's voice said, "Hi, baby." I heard Adrea pass all
the way into the room and then there was only silence. I
imagined they were miming to each other, trying to communicate; maybe Adrea was thirsty or not feeling well.

I let myself in the front door and inched down the foyer
to the opening of the living room. I wanted to see what my
mother would do. I wanted my mother to be with my child.
I waited.

And then I was surprised by the sound of my mother's
fingers, briskly on the keys, showing the first set of chords.
I knew what song it was. She played it several times as I
smiled in the shadows. I heard Adrea's attempt, I knew it
was Adrea because one key was held down too long, but the

order was perfect. Her memory was like that; she could repeat back five chords in a row on first seeing them, but my mother didn't know that.

Then my mother played the set again, adding the second set of chords. She only did it once, and Adrea played it back to her. They sounded the same. I heard my mother laugh, saying, "So good." She played the first four sets of chords, up to the chorus, and I knew the song as Adrea played it back to her. I heard them shifting positions, and then my mother started from the beginning, playing hard against the keyboard and singing.

I peeked into the room. Adrea's feet were firmly planted on the piano bench, her head and chest, arms and palms, stretched out along the top of the piano. She stood with her cheek pressed against the top of the piano, looking down at my mother. She was nodding her head and smiling. My mother played to her, playing hard to make vibrations strong enough to reach Adrea, but her singing was to herself.

> I've looked at clouds from both sides now
> From up and down, and still somehow
> It's clouds illusions I recall,
> I really don't know clouds at all.

She played the whole song, humming and singing alternately, and I knew that she was back in another time. Her face had gone back to her younger face, again sharp and narrow. She was happier than she could be with me. She was the way she used to be with us, two daughters.

She sang the chorus,

> I've looked at life from both sides now
> From win and lose and still somehow
> It's life's illusions I recall
> I really don't know life at all.

They remained at the piano, my mother's back still straight as always on the bench. I couldn't go rest my hand on her shoulder, sit beside her, although I pictured the scene as if I had.

Starting with Megan's death, the interactions I've had with my mother have lived in two versions. The way it happened, and the way I imagine it would have played out if Megan hadn't died. Even in the instant in which Megan was dying, I experienced two simultaneous versions.

I was standing on the shore watching, I did nothing, and time and nature moved forward around me.

I entered the water. Megan surfaced, her face emerging from the frothy waves. She came back to us. We grabbed her. We all came out of the water. Maybe because I believed this second version was imminent, I only waited, waited for the desired happy ending.

I stepped carefully out of the room. I edged my way along the wall away from them.

We went to see Bonnie's twins, Madeline and Samuel, their first week home from the hospital. It was the last week of summer and Adrea would be starting second grade at the Huntington School the following week. Adrea leaned over the two of them stretched out on the daybed, silently examining their small robust bodies. She placed a hand on one chest, her thumb tucked in the underarm, and rocked the baby up and down on its back. The infant raised its arms at Adrea and gasped a half smile. At a younger age Adrea would have asked me if the babies were deaf. Now she knows there is no reason they would be, it is not a fifty-fifty possibility as she once assumed, and she knows that deaf is always mentioned; hearing goes without saying.

I sat on the couch reading. Adrea had just gone to sleep for the night. Bonnie was in the shower, and Simon had come home from work, said hello, and gone to look in on his five-pound children. He entered the living room, one swaddled infant in his arms, and sat on the couch across from me, smiling his gap-toothed grin. I smiled back. "Who's that there?"

"I have no idea," he laughed. "Having twins is the best thing for a forty-year-old man. Do you know what happens to men at forty? Biologically, well, maybe it's psychosomatic, but there are many unexplained medical conditions that assail forty-year-old men and then mysteriously go away."

I heard a soft wail rising in the next room. "What are your symptoms?"

"Ah, that's Madeline, wanna go get her?"

I pushed myself out of the armchair and strode toward the bedroom. Simon called, "She's in the middle of the crib; you can't miss her."

I carried her back to the living room, encountering Bonnie wrapped in her towel. She kissed Madeline's pink face. Simon said, "Are you still growing, Anna? How tall are you? Isn't she beautiful?"

"I've always been tall."

Bonnie said, "Yes, stand up Simon, back to back, I'll measure." Surprisingly, he did, walking around me to lean against my back. Bonnie flattened his hair. They were definitely becoming odder with the arrival of the twins. I thought of my parents and Carla, Bonnie's mother, and the free random antics that took place before Megan's death. Simon was taller, inspiring him to declare, "I must be very tall and handsome."

I shook my head at their silliness. "So, what are these forty-year-old symptoms?"

He held his son in one arm, raised the other hand, pointer finger leading, "My heart raced, I was dizzy, lightheaded. It was mostly this incredible dreaminess though. Also, I couldn't remember little things throughout the day, what I was doing, and the rest of my memory flooded in, great waves of the forgotten."

Bonnie said, "I'm going to get dressed." She headed back to the bedroom, wrapping the towel around her head, exposing her white buttocks to us. She slapped herself, tossing a silly smile over her shoulder at me.

I sat back in my chair, staring into Madeline's face. She looked in my direction, unfocused, and shook her small head.

"You know, I had similar symptoms before adopting Adrea."

Bonnie and Simon, Adrea and I, were cooking dinner together. The lights were all up, the room warm and bright. Bonnie was making a fuss over preparing a whole chicken. I sat at her desk in the kitchen, my face grown stern with aggravation. At the moment, Adrea was feigning innocence, quietly wiping the utensils from the drying rack. I tried to read the recipe for a sponge cake, pretending not to watch her. Every few minutes she wandered from the kitchen to the living room, dangerously approaching the babies' room. She did a little jig, making noise with her feet on the floor; drummed two spoons; made popping sounds with her mouth. If she saw a wakeful movement from either crib, she would come running back to the kitchen, a safe distance from the disturbance. She'd woken the babies at six that morning, wanting to feed them by herself. I grew exhausted watching her play around. It's enough, I thought, I don't owe this child my entire night. I called over to Simon, "Tap Adrea for me." He drummed two fingers on the top of her head and pointed to me. She looked over, scowling already at being disciplined.

"Time for bed, A."

"No it isn't, it's early."

"You've been up since dawn, so it's time for bed."

She threw her dish towel toward me; it flapped down ineffectively a foot away from her shoes. I reacted immediately. I was out of my chair and across the kitchen gripping her arm in one movement. I heard Bonnie gasp from her place by the oven. "Enough," I said aloud to all of them. Before I let go of her arm to sign, I spoke into her face: "You are acting very poorly, you are not in charge here." There was something intentionally cruel about this. Part of her punishment was not to know what I was saying. I released her, signing, "You're going to bed now, say good night, let's go." My two hands remained extended, pointing toward the door. For a long moment she stared at them, her chin set to one side. I felt my posture, my back bent over to her height, my arms forward; my body ached. I wanted to straighten up and relax but couldn't. I started to say "Come on," but she dismissed me and the room with a wave of her hand and departed.

Standing in the bathroom doorway while she washed, I watched her straight back, her hand turning the faucets; my mind wandered away from the situation completely. I could hardly remember the emotion of the kitchen; in my mind she was already in bed, I just had to go through a few minutes of pantomime, a choreography of motions, and then I could return to something, I myself didn't know what.

I knelt on the floor next to her sleeping bag while she got in. She zippered it all the way up, scrunching down into it, her arms, chest, and head remaining outside. I sat back on my feet. She looked at my thighs in the dark room, where my hands rested, silent, and closed her eyes. I closed my eyes too. I pictured a small stone bridge passing over the Seine, a twin-headed lamppost glowing like a beacon. I thought of Katrice standing in her kitchen, her hands full of cooking items, and briefly I envisioned my mother stepping into a cab, waving good-bye.

Pablo had just returned to New York, and I would see him as soon as we were back. Three months had passed since our trip, since we'd seen each other. I was full of nervous anticipation. I opened my eyes and laid my hand on top of Adrea's. She turned away, tucking both hands under her cheek, already half asleep or still mad. I got up and left the room.

The words that Adrea can pronounce are common, everyday words: "good," "thank you," "bye-bye," and when unusual words are spoken and fingerspelled, they often join her vocabulary. I heard her say "Halloween" in a funny, forestlike voice.

Even as Adrea became more proficient in lip-reading, she continued to describe it as learning, not doing it. She enjoyed paying attention to oral movement, but being oral is controversial. I know adults who can lip-read who claim they cannot. She was not ashamed or guilty about learning anything. Yet she still used her voice only occasionally; she still opted for sign over speech. This, in the end, felt right to me. Yet I confess I got a rush when she spoke, because I could pick out her voice in a room full of others, because I knew the voice of my child. When she spoke, I imagined that an utterly fine feeling possessed her. I believed it was an adventurous impulse, like a young fox popping out of its den because the day is inviting.

Since returning from France, Martin had been working part-time at the Hearing Center. It was gratifying to offer him the opportunity and to watch him with the children. Martin had arranged a CPR training course for all the teachers. The trainers came to the school one evening. Adrea drew and read in the book corner while we took the training. The teachers had been talking about the course a lot, in speech and sign, C-P-R.

A few days after the course there was an epidemic in our fish tank. Every morning we encountered more dead fish.

We all began a close scrutiny of the fifty-five gallon tank. Whenever passing the tank, the kids and teachers would stop and peer in, examining the condition of the remaining fish. All morning we'd been watching one sickly fish hiding behind a plant. There was great suspicion that he was the next to go. When the fated fish did approach his death, Martin, Adrea, and I were all peering into the tank. The fish darted out from the plant in a last burst of health and swam for the surface, then lost all energy and began to sink to the bottom, upside down, his gills pumping with sharp efforts. He drifted down to the gravel and lay there upside-down. Adrea held her arms out stiffly, her thumbs pointing together, pressing, and said, "Cee-Bee-Ar."

It took the fish about five minutes to die. I began to really consider pressing its tiny, scaled body back into life. Its gills opened and shut painfully, as if it didn't belong in water. I watched the bright red blinking of its gills, hoping it would die soon.

I went to Pablo's apartment. We'd had one awkward phone conversation since his return. Standing outside his front door, I found the same old feelings rising up in me, friendship, desire, and fear, as though I were not a human being with intelligent emotions but just a physical place where feelings were caught up. It was a very hot September day, and when he opened the door the comfort of his apartment returned to me as a visceral memory. His apartment was ten degrees cooler than outside; it seemed to generate its own cool draft. Pablo looked tall to me, wearing shorts and a T-shirt, no shoes. I smiled and gave a short wave. He smiled back and stretched out his arm, welcoming me into his apartment.

Pablo had lived in the same apartment for many years, a loft: the kitchen, living room, study, and bedroom all laid out within one vast room. The space was painted several shades of blue. There was one giant window, ten by ten feet, a grid of one hundred small panes; a rectangle of them in the middle could be pulled in to open the window. The view was of the East River.

In the evening, facing out that window, feeling a breeze and hearing a distant foghorn, it was as though I were not on the sixth floor of an old factory building but in the blue steel hull of a ship pushing forward.

The lure of the place caught me, and the otherworldliness of it, and the desire to stay and leave everything else behind. I sat on his plain gray couch, Pablo beside me.

"How are you?" I asked.

"Happy to be home."

I thought of the guest room he'd inhabited in his mother's apartment, the suffocating coverlet on the tiny bed, the pile of his books on the floor, not a writing surface in the whole place. I hadn't realized how oppressed he'd appeared in those reduced surroundings. Now he seemed inflated by his natural habitat. We generally spent more time at my apartment than his because of Adrea. I felt the presence of his ex-girlfriend, Lindsay, who had lived in this space with him.

"I feel as if I haven't seen you for a long time," I said nervously. "Paris seems unreal, like a dream."

"It was real—" He started to speak but stopped and looked at me. "I'm having a hard time, Anna. It feels right to be together again." He glanced at me. "I'm thinking about our future. Are you?"

I nodded, feeling the pressure of having finally reached this pinnacle.

"I love you," he said plainly.

"Pablo, I don't know why it's so hard for me. I get so awkward and scared. I want to be with you. It's just the whole world is such an out-of-control place, and we're bobbing around in it with no self-determination."

"I know you struggle with it, Anna. But we all do it somehow, live in it." He stretched his legs out on the couch toward me. I squeezed his feet, then, pushing him toward the inside, I stretched out alongside him; we faced each other, resting our heads on the sofa's opposite arms.

"My life has always felt so accidental. But I want to be decisive about us." My voice was urgent in my own ears.

He laid his hand down on top of my foot, feeling the curved bone there. Then he took it away. There was palpable tension.

After a long silence, I continued, "Megan used to hold my father's hand all the time, the hand with the wedding ring. If I was holding his hand, she asked me to switch so she could hold the ringed hand. His hand with that wedding ring, it's as if she were drawn to solid things, a gold ring and her father's grip, things she could hold on to."

Pablo sat up and flipped around on the sofa to wrap his arms around me from behind. I lay with my back against his chest and Pablo rocked me. I felt his breath move in and out, and I matched mine to it.

BOOK FOUR

―――――――⟋e⟍―――――――

My kitchen was full of light. The sun moved through in thick layers, landing on different surfaces, illuminating the floating dust. The phone in my hand became a long-lost sea creature. I searched for something to latch on to. My own kitchen, a full coffee press giving off a curl of steam, the beginnings of the dinner I was making, appointment reminders and Adrea's artwork taped to the refrigerator.

My father's voice came at me, not through the telephone, the telephone had been transformed, his voice came from the doorway, or window, or from a movie screen, scratchy and hollow, the word "suicide." The room tilted sharply to one side, grew dark. I don't remember.

Maritza had keys and let herself in. She and Adrea had been playing in the park. They arrived flushed from the brisk autumn air. She shook me. The kitchen floor was so comfortable supporting my head. I told Maritza I was okay, I spoke to her on and on, not acknowledging I was using the wrong language. "Some bad news, I'm okay, let me lie here a moment." Adrea hovered over me. I tried to piece it together—I must have fainted on the phone.

I started crying out loud. I tried not to, I covered my mouth. Maritza was horrified; Adrea looked truly scared. I sat up and leaned against the cupboards, pushed my hair back behind my ears, and signed to Maritza, "My father called, my mother" . . . what is the sign for suicide, how did she kill herself? "My mother killed herself." Maritza's face crumpled. I stood up shakily, wanting to take control. Adrea stared at me. She came and wrapped her arms around my waist, pressing her head into my stomach. Briefly, I put my arms around her shoulders, squeezed.

"Maritza, do you think you could take Adrea for a few nights? I need to go to California, to my father. I don't want her missing school." Maritza nodded. She removed Adrea from me, as I was already walking out of the kitchen, heading to Adrea's room to pack her clothes.

I grabbed a large suitcase out of the hall closet and dropped it in front of Adrea's dresser. Maritza and Adrea stood in the doorway watching me pull out her clothes. I signed, "I'm going to get a late-night flight. I'll be gone about a week. Maritza, is that okay, please, can you take her?" Adrea came and hugged my waist again. I stroked her hair, looking at Maritza.

"If you want me to, fine, of course."

"Thank you." I pulled Adrea back, saying, "Help me pack, okay?" She nodded bravely. "I'm going to help Grandpa. I think it would be better for you to stay with Maritza." She nodded again, and we packed her clothes in silence. My mother had pushed me away in her pain, when I was a child and ultimately now. I felt the tendency in my own bones, the distance I needed to survive. My mother did this. But there is no other way to do it.

A new layer in the rock formation. I hadn't thought of it in years, but all of that time my father and mother were yet something new. Adrea and I were also a period in time, marked by our own combination of elements. The newest geological shift would be stark and could not yet be seen.

What is not made of memory is nothing. The present does not exist, I fear, because of the way we shirk through it. Not one of us knows how to move our body, draw air into our lungs, without comparing it to the last movement, last breath. And the stories that are the past, which is all there is, are elusive. How do you tame or whittle or lure one memory into telling the truth? Show me how to look at a child without seeing another child, or its mother, or the place where she came from.

My father picked me up at the San Francisco airport. He drove slowly, placing his hand on my shoulder at each stop. I tried to form a question in my mind, nothing fitting together coherently. "There will be people arriving tomorrow," he said, "Carla, and Bonnie's bringing the twins. I figured you'd like that."

"I will. I spoke to Bonnie briefly today," I assured him, feeling the emptiness of the backseat looming behind me. I forced myself not to turn and look. I pictured my mother and my sister, sitting straight in their seats, their heads fallen back in a good-postured sleep.

I wanted to ask how my mother killed herself. Searching fruitlessly for other, benign questions, I unsuccessfully tried to avoid this one. After a long silence I said, "Dad, can I ask you how she did it?"

He was stopped at a light and turned to look at me, seeming to question my timing, but no: "I'm sorry, love, I thought I told you. She took all her pills." He accelerated too quickly when the light changed, making the tires squeal. "She's been taking valium again."

Her visit to see me in New York was almost four months prior. "How long has she been back on medication?" I asked.

"This past year."

I gazed out my window until we were stopped in front of the house. My parents lived in the same house in Berkeley that the three of us moved into after Megan's death. The house's exterior used to be shades of brown; they had repainted it gray and white, I wondered when. I had spent no more than five nights there since my second year of college.

We parked in the driveway. I wanted to take a walk through the quiet streets before entering the house, which I feared would swallow me whole. I stood on the curb and turned left, then right, feeling so familiar in what used to be my territory. How quickly I had left my adult life and Deaf life; the hearing world is always so huge and ready to rise up around you. Entering the house, I was compelled to walk straight through it, out to the backyard; I resisted being confined by those walls. I resisted going back to our shared past. Something was telling me that I wouldn't have any choice, that I risked losing myself there. Fate has always been stronger than I am.

Finally I walked around in the downstairs rooms, grazing my shoulder or fingertips along the walls, window to window. What could not be changed by new paint or furniture was what the house had always been to me—the view outside. One window framed a silver pine pressed against the glass, denser and taller than before; another window showed bamboo stalks, the narrow side yard glimpsed between. Just as I did as a lonely girl, I veered from one window to the next, finding something comforting from outside of us.

I found myself in the tight surroundings of my mother's closet, pressed between two racks of her hanging clothes. What will my father do with her clothes, her personal things? It was a practical thought, but what I felt was panic. I left the closet and went to their bed. I sat carefully on her side. Did my father make the bed that morning, after waking up alone for the first time, before driving to the airport for his adult daughter, to bury his wife?

I noticed the phone by the bed. It seemed like a lifeline that could pull me out of there when I needed to get out. I had called Pablo after my father's call the day before, but I didn't have the words to leave a message. Now I hesitated. I didn't know if I should ask him to come. I dialed the number. He picked up on the second ring, and gratitude washed over me.

"Hi, it's me. I'm in California at my parents' house." My voice broke, and the rest came out more air than words. "My mother committed suicide yesterday."

"Oh my God, Anna."

"My dad called, and I just got on a red-eye flight. Pablo . . . I don't know what to do. I can't believe this is what she wanted."

"Wanted?" he asked. I repeated myself as if he hadn't heard me. "I don't know about that, Anna." He was silent and so was I. "I'm so sorry, I'm shocked. . . . Anna?"

"I'm here," I said.

"She must have been very unhappy," Pablo continued. "She probably felt she had no choice."

"I know she was really unhappy. I can't believe she could do this to my father, and me." Now he was silent. "Pablo, I know it's a lot, it's okay if you can't, but I was wondering if you could come out here?"

"Yes, I can come."

"I'm so grateful, thank you, Pab. Being here in this house, my childhood feels so close." I picked up a small candle next to her bed and dragged it across the white wall. It left a mark. I drew a wave on the wall and then another and another.

"I'll call you back," Pablo said, "let me check about a flight for tomorrow."

I stopped drawing. "Okay, and thank you. You know, she was probably more depressed after seeing me in New York."

We got off the phone for Pablo to check flights.

I dropped the candle in the wastebasket and returned to her closet. Her smell was everywhere, on all of her clothes. I took out a suit and pressed it against me, a thick wool I know she wore to class. I realized how frail her body had looked in New York. Were these clothes like costumes to her? Items used for passing? Each day rising from sleep, she'd put on the necessary wardrobe to pass in the world.

My father yelled up from the bottom of the stairs, the telephone was for me. I stepped out of the closet feeling displaced by his voice, unsure of my whereabouts. I saw the forgotten candle marks on the wall, a series of waves. For an instant, I wondered where they came from, then I was ashamed. I picked up the phone.

"Hello." My voice was small.

"Anna, I can arrive at four tomorrow. Will you pick me up or should I take a cab?

"I'll pick you up. It'll be a full house—Bonnie and the babies and Carla."

"Good. It's good to have people around. How's Adrea?"

For the first time since arriving I thought of Adrea. "I didn't bring her, I left her with Maritza." I hadn't questioned this decision at all. "I didn't want her in this house."

"I understand. Will you be okay today?"

"Yeah, I'm going to go be with my dad."

"Okay, I'll see you tomorrow love."

I put down the phone as quietly as possible. Reaching up, I scratched at one of the waxy blue marks with my nail. Why hadn't I heard the phone ring? I picked it up and turned it on its side. The ringer was off. I picked at the button with my finger, not switching it. Did my mother turn it off? Very clearly, I saw her forefinger in the exact place as my own. How many things right then were just as she had left them?

I found my father downstairs in the kitchen; I told him that Pablo was coming the next day, in the afternoon. He answered, "Carla and Bonnie will be here in the morning. I'll go pick them up, they get in very early."

"Okay, Dad." He put his arms around me. He pressed his cheek against the top of my head. I felt self-conscious, as if I were the recipient of some misdirected affection. The last time we shared the rituals of mourning, he and my mother were like a pair of doves together, and I was alone or paired with Grandma. By default, I have become my father's chosen one.

I slept later than usual. When I came downstairs in the morning, I saw Carla, Bonnie, and the babies seated in the backyard with my father. Bonnie held one baby, her mother the other. I stared. The configuration was all changed. Once it had been my parents and Carla and three little girls. Carla noticed me; she smiled and rose, handing my father the sleeping baby. She headed toward me, reaching for me. As Carla took me in her arms, I looked at Bonnie, holding her daughter, smiling sadly at me. Time was collapsing, the past merging with the present.

The kitchen was full of food baskets my father had received. My father and Carla and I settled in the living room. Carla sat on the couch and shook her head at the additional food baskets my father had left on the coffee table. My father settled next to her and pushed the baskets around aimlessly.

Carla rubbed her temples with her eyes closed. I turned to go in pursuit of Bonnie and the children, but my father's abrupt sobbing stopped me. His face fell forward into his hands. He shook. Carla and I both reached to comfort him.

I couldn't accept that she had left him. The rest of us,

the rest of the world, yes, but not him. That he was broken and ruined like this and she inflicted it was impossible. My father, still covering his face with both hands, chanted, "Why, why, why?"

I touched him gently. His shoulder was solid and tense. He grew quiet and dried his face with a handkerchief. He thanked us and went into the bathroom.

Carla said, "Anna, I want to talk with you privately."

We went upstairs to my childhood bedroom. She was my mother's age. She pulled up the blind on the window. She looked outside, at the front lawn, the street, her back to me. It had started to rain.

"This wasn't about you, Anna. We all have to think that way. I can't even imagine that she thought of me at all. Because, had she thought of me, wouldn't she have turned to me for help?"

"That's not something I need to wonder about."

Carla turned from the window. "Anna, you think your mother got no happiness from you?"

"We haven't been close my whole adult life. I know I made her unhappy."

"By growing up to be a good person, a loving mother to Adrea, you made her feel worthwhile."

"She told you that?" I asked.

"She didn't have to."

I could only wave my hand, shake my head. I didn't know what effect I'd had on my mother. To relieve Carla, I said, "I know she didn't do this because of me."

"No, not because of any of us."

Our silence filled the room. Carla seemed calmer; she had said what she needed to. I sat straight on the edge of the bed. She stood staring out the window, but I imagined she was looking inward, at the way things had turned out for all of us. I thought about how long they'd been friends, almost my whole lifetime, Bonnie's lifetime, so far past

Megan. Carla sat on the bed beside me, rubbed her hand lightly on my thigh.

Carla spoke to me softly. "Anna, I went into your mother's room. The wall," slowly, with compassion, "I don't think you meant anything by it, but it will upset your father to see it . . . we need to clean the wall."

I moved down the hall in a daze. My father was sitting on his bed gazing up at the desecrated wall. "Dad, I'm sorry. I didn't know what I was doing. I was on the phone, I wasn't thinking. I'm going to clean it off."

He didn't look at me, he was staring at the cartoonish waves; they had him mesmerized. "But, what is it?"

Carla was behind me again; she poked a spray bottle of cleanser and a rag into my hand. I started cleaning the candle wax off the wall farthest away from where my father's attention was focused. The mark vanished; I kept working, Carla left us, my father continued to sit and watch me erase.

I sat next to him. "Dad, where did you find her?"

"She took the pills and got in the bathtub." He gestured toward their master bathroom.

I shuddered, feeling the close proximity to where we sat on the bed.

"She fell asleep and never woke up, gone." He'd grown calm or was numbed.

We sat together silently.

I waited at the curb for Pablo to emerge from the terminal. I stared straight out, my hands resting in my lap like dead weights.

I didn't see Pablo until he tried the passenger door; it was locked. I leaned over to open it. His face hung outside the window for an instant, he smiled at me. I tried smiling back. He got into the car. I continued to sit there, not ready to start the car and drive home.

After studying my profile, he said, "Anna, come here.

You're so gone." He pulled my tense shoulders into his chest. His body was too human for me. I could smell his clean hair, and he was giving off an impossible degree of heat. Our bodies refused to bond together, as though two full strangers were pushed into each other. I said, "Thanks for coming." He still held me. "You're welcome." I told myself to behave better.

My father was genuinely happy to see Pablo. He complimented him on his last collection of poems, pointed out the volume on the shelf. Carla treated him as a handsome gentleman guest, she catered to him sweetly. Bonnie presented the babies. Pablo asked to hold Samuel and lifted him from Bonnie's arms. While being gently rocked, Samuel smiled brightly at this new stranger. Here was a man not broken, not in grief, to lay one's affections on.

He had flown across the country to be with me, and I was scared he would regret it, the entire situation being too intense, and me too needy. After we'd had a light supper, I told Pablo that I'd bring his bag upstairs; he followed me.

My old bedroom had been converted into a guest room. Pablo stepped into the room behind me. I placed his bag by the bedside. He spread his hand over his breast, a physical habit of contemplation.

"Remember sleeping in this room after our freshman year?"

He nodded, smiling gently. "I do."

I covered my face with my hands; with effort I didn't allow the tears, afraid of taking advantage of his comfort. I raised my head again, forcing a smile.

Pablo came toward me and for the second time wrapped his arms around me. I clung on this time, feeling like my body belonged there.

"Let's go to bed early, you look wasted," he said.

We lay fully dressed on my childhood bed, and I let everything drift away from me. Both my parents became some distant image. The room, life in New York, the Center, myself as a mother, became distant places on the horizon.

And who should be in the room with us but Megan. Her little spirit flitted about.

I lay with my head on Pablo's shoulder and felt the first calmness come over me since I stood in my kitchen, before I got the news.

Megan hovered. I longed for daylight and to be outdoors. I longed for brightness to flood in and this bird-child sister to float around me for the rest of my life, which would be only daytime. I wished to banish all night.

The room at the funeral home was smallish, with dark wood pews, a stage containing the dark-stained coffin, closed and to remain closed. There were no flowers; there were prayer books in front of every seat in the pocket shelf. The room was crowded. I sat in the second pew with Pablo, Bonnie, and Carla beside me; my father and my uncle Ben were in front of us. People filed in through the doors, so many that I didn't think everyone would fit in the room. They entered and looked toward the front of the room, looking for the real mourners, the shivah sitters, the people Carolyn did this to.

As people spotted me, I imagined they quickly averted their eyes and moved into the pews, sliding all the way down, scooting in. They pressed their legs against each other. All crammed in, like the animals in Noah's ark, needing to make room. The doorway never cleared, they kept coming in, people from the university, from back East, distant relatives, family friends. My father tapped my knee. I jerked around, startled. He squeezed my hand and turned back to the front. I guessed he wanted me to stop staring back at the door. Pablo took my hand in both of his and held it. I kept my eyes on our hands pressed together. I could barely feel them.

An hour earlier, my father and I had sat with the rabbi, telling him about my mother so he could conduct the service as if he'd known her. My father seemed too willing to oblige this charade. He sat there as I imagine a man sits before a loan officer at a bank trying not to seem desperate. Of course he told the rabbi about Megan. He could not describe my mother's identity without the defining factor of losing Megan. Losing her child was who my mother was.

My father reported that my mother was very loyal. She handled her commitments to the university with seriousness and attention to detail. "The qualifications are . . . ," chimed in my head. My father described her tendency toward solitude: "She didn't pursue friends, not that she had none or didn't care for them, but it was usually just the two of us. Probably she preferred to be totally alone." This wasn't describing my mother's true nature, this was a description of a mourner, my mother of the last twenty-eight years, but not her natural way of being. He said nothing about music, about the long loping rush of her body running, the way she spun her daughters in big arcing circles around her, her huge openmouthed laughs, because that woman was buried in a coffin the size of a five-year-old.

As my father continued about her inclination toward hard work and solitude, he leaned in toward the rabbi; his shoulders rounding submissively, trying to convey her depression, I realized he was making an apology and hoping for her to be forgiven before she was buried. My father confided, "My wife took her own life." The rabbi looked sympathetic. "Yes, I know that." My father leaned even farther forward; his eyes were imploring. He was trying to seduce forgiveness. The rabbi said, "What else do you want to tell me?" His eyes moved between us.

"Most people hold on to life as long as possible," I said, "I believe she did too."

My father's eulogy surprised and moved me. What I thought we'd all agreed on, the omnipotence of fate, the thoughtless plan of the planet, he was now giving meaning to.

"What choices are ours?" my father said. "It is generally accepted that we do not choose when to be born, when to die. My Carolyn gained courage and peace from imagining that our young daughter, a quarter of a century ago, on a narrow strip of beach at the age of five, may have with some divine knowledge chosen her own time to go. Maybe our child had been merely visiting us, a messenger, a message, a spirit in our midst? Maybe we do choose when to be born. Maybe, like a star falling in the night sky, some conscious particle of the soul pitches itself forward, binding itself to a human story, making the choice, volunteering at the exact right moment of a mortal conception, saying, 'Yes, I.'"

"These are the things I say to comfort myself," my father continued. "I have lost half of my family, my daughter Megan and my wife, Carolyn. I know no reasons for their painful departures from this living world. But I blame them not, and if death was something my Carolyn chose, I say she must have known something I can't."

I lay on the couch downstairs. Samuel was stretched out long on top of me. He was asleep, his small stomach pressing breaths into my rib cage. One little hand was flung up, touching my cheek. I traced circles on his face, in his hair. I was listening to Bonnie talk to a small group of guests, but I wasn't really following her words. My head was twisted sideways to watch Bonnie's face. Her expression shifted effortlessly with the telling of her story.

I bent my head to see Samuel's dear face, utterly gentle and pure. Whatever good there might be in the world was all contained in that one small human for me, that breathing, pumping, omniscient, and ignorant babe. Practicing my deafness, I tuned out Bonnie's voice, focused only on everyone's faces, the colors of the room, the changing light. Carla was very still, listening to her daughter. I had been noticing all the things Bonnie did for her mother: she shut the window, turned off the flame under the kettle, fetched her mother's sweater for her. I would never do anything for my mother again, and before, I did so little.

Pablo had left that morning, taking with him the one small part of me that felt connected to the world. My father noticed the difference, saying, "He puts some light in your eyes." It was true, and I cupped that feeling tight, keeping it close.

At the end of the week, a day before my departure, my father came into my bedroom to tell me there was a call from New York Relay. I expected it was Maritza checking in.

I said to the operator, "Hi, this is Anna." The operator typed to the caller and then waited for a typed response to read to me. I waited. The operator said, "Hi Mommy. I miss you, I'm fine, how are you?" Tears came to my eyes, I had never felt so distant from Adrea before. I stammered to the operator, "Hi, sweetie. Have you been a good girl for Maritza?" I waited again for Adrea's response; her typing would be slow. I felt my heart beating.

"I've been good. I went to the movies with Maritza, we made lasagña and rice and beans. I made you a present at school." The operator's voice was monotone.

"I'm coming home tomorrow. We can talk more then. I love you."

Hanging up, I couldn't imagine my life in New York. The life I'd created was out of focus; something felt cut off. I didn't feel a strong pull to bring me back home, almost as though there had been a one-way surge of energy that had brought me where I was, in my parent's house. I was not the same woman I was before, not the same Anna of seven days earlier. I didn't want to go home, to everything that waited there for me, even Adrea.

My mother had weighed the effect of her death on my father and me against her own pain and chosen herself. That is a mother who doesn't love in the usual way. Or worse, I am a child who didn't conjure the usual love. But, I thought perhaps she had waited until now, for me. Perhaps she had held back all of these years until I was ready to be without her. But I was eight when she removed herself from me. I've worried about the distance I allowed to lengthen between us, but it wasn't my allowing it but rather learning to live with it. Perhaps it is not at all useful to measure the ages or dates or duration of love refused.

My father needed this week to end. I saw, with each friend's departure, more air being allowed in. He was becoming lighter. And my departure could be the most dramatic and lightening. It felt unnecessary to say how we were feeling; there would be time. My father would be all right. He would survive. He didn't resemble the shell of a man that looked for Megan continuously. He moved among the living, tears often coursing down his cheeks, his shoulders suddenly collapsing, his face hidden behind his hands, but still, he was with us.

I opened the front door of my apartment. It felt empty and unwelcoming. I sat in my living room like a visitor. Eventually I pushed off my shoes and curled up in the armchair, covering myself with my coat as a blanket. The windows were bare and for the first time looked exposed and unfriendly to me; they revealed the black of night. Where did I fit into this night, this city, this life?

When I woke up still in the chair, it was midnight. The room was cold, and my legs were stiff. I needed to call Maritza and Adrea. They knew I was returning that day, so it couldn't be put off any longer. Looking at my watch, I knew that Adrea would be long asleep. I dialed on the TTY, picturing Maritza seated in her own living room, the lamp by her chair, and others in her kitchen and bedroom, flickering on and off, indicating the ringing phone. She picked up quickly. After saying hello, I confessed that it didn't feel great to be back home, maybe too final or something.

Maritza's typed messages were abrupt.

"It's too soon, you must be very sad."

Her deaf bluntness caused me to be more honest. "I'm not good. I need to talk to you in person. Can I come over now?"

"Of course. (smile) I thought maybe you'd say you don't want to come now. We really want to see you."

"Maritza, don't wake up Adrea. I need to talk to you first." I wanted to type the smile, but I knew it wasn't in my voice, it would be false. "Okay?"

"Yes, Okay. She's asleep."

I knelt on the floor to lean up against the bed, so as not to wake her. She smelled like candy. I wanted to breathe her in, wrap my hands around her head and narrow shoulders and press her into me. I wanted to have her in my arms, but I didn't touch her.

I turned away. Seated on the floor with my back against the mattress, I felt my stomach heave and clench, and then I was crying so loudly, I thought at first I was hearing someone else cry. My nose ran and hot tears poured from my eyes; I cried as I hadn't since I was a child.

Maritza appeared in the doorway. She flinched at the sight of me.

After I had washed my face and composed myself, I returned to the same doorway. With my eyes only, I examined all the evidence of Adrea. Her suitcase was open in the corner, a new package of underwear torn open on the floor.

A workbook and a pile of colored pencils, shoes, socks, books, hair bands, all the items of a life, a girl, made my heart race. I couldn't incorporate those things. I felt driven away by the day-to-day living a human life requires.

We sat in Maritza's living room and had a cup of tea. She said, "You need more time to relax." The word "relax" struck me as extremely simple. I concentrated on the sign. It is the same gesture as happy, except happy is two hands on opposite sides of the chest, brushing up, outward from the body, open. Relax crosses the palms and pats the feeling inward to the body, like bringing happiness inside, excluding others. I would have liked to be alone, and away, and be happy.

I did take Adrea home. Not that night, but the next day. I put fresh sheets on both our beds. I stocked the refrigerator. I practiced normal expressions in the mirror. My smile was a false molding attached to a wall. Like any other ailment, I knew it would be observed by Adrea.

When I picked her up and brought her home in a cab and walked up the street with her to our apartment, I realized I was not prepared for the reality of her, for how a child can change in ten days. In her calm posture upon first seeing me, her giving glances and carefulness, I saw myself at the exact same age, following a different death. It endeared and frightened me more with her. I knew this child would do anything for me, give it all, require nothing. I wanted to say something to put her at ease, to reassure her. But it wasn't possible for me.

Later, I kissed her good night, tucked the blanket under her chin. She declined a story; had she outgrown stories in ten days? I said, "I love you." That wasn't hard; it was certainly true. But saying more, explaining my feelings, I couldn't. I feared that Adrea could read all of my thoughts, that she could see them turning out from my mind, repeatedly, "I can't, I can't." And innocent Adrea was part of it.

She was the biggest part in the life that I suddenly thought I could no longer do.

I took Adrea to the Hearing Center. She joined her classes obediently. She required nothing; she was as easy as not even being. I recognized the device. My heart went out to her, but mostly I was grateful. I puttered at my desk. I cleaned my entire office, enjoying the work of spraying Windex, wiping surfaces clean. That kind of work I could do. I planned to clean the entire Center and our apartment; I plotted all the chores. Maritza came upstairs to look in on me. I was relieved by her smile—I wasn't doing too little yet. She went back to the next class without mentioning that I wasn't teaching my class. They would cover for me; it's natural after a death. But I feared I would never return to it.

That night I cleaned compulsively, calming myself with the thoroughness. I peeked in her doorway and saw Adrea unpacking. Her movements were so deliberate, so mature; I imagined her being quick, thoughtless, accidental, a child. We cleaned together and stopped for dinner, and our night passed. We prepared for bed. Adrea allowed me these activities without communication.

Each night that week, after school and work, we sat on the couch, Adrea's head in my lap, and we watched television. I stroked her hair back from her forehead, enjoying her weight on me. We watched the TV on mute, neither of us very interested. Adrea absorbed my touch, making it somehow enough. And her catlike satisfaction with a mere hand to rub against didn't overwhelm me, allowed me to pass that first terrible week.

On the weekend we went grocery shopping together. In the store I picked out the items we always kept in the house. There was a little boy with his mother; we seemed to be following their cart with our own. He repeatedly picked out appealing-looking items and begged for them. His mother was in a good mood. Yes, he could have it. I wasn't really paying attention to them as we slowly followed their cart. Adrea was watching though, and I was vaguely aware of her attention. Then she imitated the boy, picking up a colorful box of breakfast cereal, something she'd never tried. She brought it over and showed it to me, her eyebrows up in the form of a question. I nodded and took it from her hand, dropping it into our cart. We kept walking. Adrea fell back in pace with me. She had been looking for an interaction. I felt her desire for me, and I was powerless to respond. That night after she'd put herself to bed, I heard her crying. When I opened her bedroom door she pretended to sleep.

That night I lay in my bed alone in the dark. Forgotten memories came rushing at me. One Halloween my mother had picked me up from kindergarten dressed as Raggedy Ann, with a red yarn wig and giant freckles on her face, a white apron and black-and-white striped stockings. I cried because I didn't recognize her, but afterward I was proud she was my mother. Once, in high school, I got picked up by the Berkeley police for being truant. I was taken back to school, and the principal's office called my mother. She lied to the principal and said she knew I wasn't in school that day because we needed to take care of some family business. She came and picked me up and we went out to lunch. I remembered her at Megan's funeral. She dropped a fistful of dirt on the coffin. Her hair was down, and it whipped around her face. She hugged me tight. I wished I'd been able to touch her more when she was here last. I wanted to feel her embrace, and it might have made a difference. Maybe not enough of a difference, but possibly we could have reached each other.

～

We drove to Northampton to visit Bonnie. It was finally spring, and the small college town was blooming everywhere. Bonnie and I sat on the edge of her back porch, our legs stretched out in front of us in the sun. Adrea was sprawled on the lawn like a starfish. She was showing Samuel the signs for "green," "sky," "happy," "baby"; she pronounced the word with the sign. He cocked his head, finding the sound of her funny, or else surprised by her departure from silence. But he didn't hesitate long. He, in turn, was telling Adrea all the important monosyllables, "da," "go," "up," "boo." His saliva made steady drips from his chin to his naked chest and protruding belly. Adrea wiped it off sporadically, running her fingers through the grass. A long hard year had quickly passed since our trip to France, the twins were nine months.

I watched them while drinking my tea, afloat with chamomile flowers. Bonnie said, "God, look at her." I followed her eyes to Madeline. Unlike her brother, she had a small red dress on over her diaper. She was gripping the sides of an Adirondack chair, which looked more like a wooden fortress next to her small body. Bonnie said, "I admire them so much. Do you realize that almost everything they do is done with all their might?" Earlier Madeline had climbed up the front of the chair and sat posing for pictures. But this time she tried to raise herself over the arm unassisted and we watched her straining for a sort of overhanded pull-up onto the chair's broad arm, her barefoot toes barely lifting off the lawn and then falling back. She was grunting with the effort.

Her hair was dark brown and already curled at the bottom, whereas Samuel's was sandy and straight. Bonnie described how she imagined them before they were born, Madeline, a little lady in a straw hat with a ribbon and a blue sailor dress, playing with a little wild boy.

Bonnie continued, "Imagine putting all your might into all of your actions. How often do adults do something with all their might?"

I watched Madeline's totally earnest face, pursed with

her attempt to conquer the chair. I thought about what in my life I had given my all to. I learned sign language with all my might. I practiced incessantly. I always wanted to know more, why each sign was made. But that was an escape.

I had been more present, more effortful, more engaged in raising Adrea than in anything else in life. I had been committing to her as fully as I was able to commit to anyone or anything, and with pleasure. But since my mother's death I hadn't been. I wasn't giving my all anymore; I was barely able to give enough.

And the one moment in my life where my actions were most needed, the moment that continues to burn like the sun for my diminished family, that we survivors must hopelessly rotate around, I hadn't moved an inch. If only I had jumped into that water and found my sister, and life had continued as we knew it.

"Bonnie, I think it's possible I've never done anything my whole life with all my might. And I know why. I watched Megan drown in that ocean and didn't do anything, frozen solid. And now my mother too; she was with me in New York a few months before her suicide. There must have been something I could have said or done that would have changed things for her. But I'm still frozen."

I rose abruptly. Scooping Madeline out of the grass, I plopped her down in the chair she'd been trying to surmount. She rooted around happily, chattering her satisfaction with her gained arrival, however earned.

I sat beside Bonnie again, and she wrapped her arms around my shoulders. "Anna, there was nothing more you could have done." Bonnie tightened her embrace. "Not for either of them." I hugged her back, my eyes still on Madeline. "Anna, my mom is selling the house on Cape Cod. She's hardly been there at all since Megan's death. We went there right before your mom died, and she was thinking about it then. She never got over losing Megan there. She's sure she wants to sell now."

The house, the vacation house that Carla and Mannie had shared with my family. The house that I remember clearly from six straight summers, the house on the cape, the house we entered as three people, wet from the sea, destroyed by the sea, when we'd last passed through its door as four. The house I one time loved, and many times cursed.

"Can I go there?" I asked Bonnie.

Early the next morning I caught Bonnie and Simon in an intimate embrace in the kitchen. I quietly went back to the guest room, postponing my tea. It brought back a memory from when I must have been very little and had caught my own parents standing in our Boston kitchen.

My mother had been leaning against the counter. In front of her were many halved oranges, and at first I had been happy because I wanted orange juice. She was wearing her terry cloth robe, and my father was holding up the back of it around her waist. He wore nothing, and he rocked his body into hers.

I was frightened when I saw my father pressed against my mother in the kitchen, her back exposed where her body had opened and the baby had burst out, and I knew the baby was somewhere upstairs. I thought there was danger.

I cried out, "Stop it, Daddy, you're hurting Mommy." My father jumped away from my mother. Her robe fell down to the floor and she wrapped it around herself. She was laughing, and she handed my father a dish towel and he covered himself and walked past me out of the kitchen. She called me to her and said, "It's okay, sweetie. Let's go upstairs and get the baby, it must be time for breakfast."

I quietly left the guest room and went down the hall to the room where Adrea was sleeping. I opened the door just as she was sitting up in her bed.

"Hi, you're awake. How are you?" I asked her.

She signed the simple gesture GOOD, her palm moving gently away from her chin.

I sat on her bed and opened my arms, asking for a hug. She burrowed into me, her arms roped around my neck in a loose lock. She felt like part of my body, an outside heart pressing away at its work. I hugged her tight, tears of gratitude seeping out of my eyes.

Adrea let go and, leaning back on her pillow, signed, "I love Samuel."

I laughed, wiping my eyes. "They're sweet babies, right?"

"Yes," Adrea signed. "They're learning how to talk now."

I nodded. "Yes, they are. Should we get dressed and have breakfast?"

She signed and said out loud, "Okay, Mom."

I leaned over her and stroked her hair back once. "Thanks for being my girl."

She smiled, looking pleased, got out of bed, and pulled on her jeans from yesterday.

Two weeks later I told Adrea that I needed to take a special trip for a few days. I said that it had to do with my mother and my sister who died and that I had to go alone. I imagined that I was going to scatter my mother's ashes, even though we had buried her body six months ago in California red earth. When Adrea was in bed, I called Pablo.

"I'm feeling better now than I have in months. Maybe it's the spring, and we had a good time in Northampton."

"You've been sounding better lately, more like yourself," Pablo replied.

"Listen, I have to tell you something." I felt that I needed to tell Pablo directly. "I'm going to go to Cape Cod this weekend, to Carla's house at the beach. They're selling it and I want to see it one more time."

"Are you sure that's a good idea?"

"I want to go."

"Would you like me to go with you?"

"Thanks, Pablo, but no, I need to go alone."

"What about Adrea?"

"She'll stay with Maritza. Do you want to come over tonight?"

Pablo arrived an hour later. We stood in the foyer kissing. Pablo hummed while he kissed me, making me smile.

We stepped into the living room. Pablo looked around the room and then at me. He smiled and went back out into the hallway and brought in a suitcase. "I thought I'd stay here with Adrea when you go to Cape Cod. Then she can be in her own home, having a swell time with me."

I stared. "No, it's too much. I couldn't ask you to do that."

"You tell me her schedule, I can follow directions." He stretched his arms wide, palms open. "If Adrea's comfortable with it, let's do it. Let me do it."

"Are you sure?"

"Yes, it's done." He kissed me again.

As the road entered the Cape, the light itself was a memory. I recognized the purple and pink of Cape Cod daylight. I had always thought that water was the birth of creation, but suddenly I knew otherwise: before there was water there was light, because the first thing birthed in water came into light. I was thinking about beginnings as the pine trees surrounding the house loomed into sight. I parked and walked through the yard and out to the dunes without stopping. My legs carried me down the slope of beach to where the sand seemed damp and cool, and I began walking down the beach, blinded by the sun.

Upon returning to the house, I turned on all the lights, circling through the three connected downstairs rooms. The wood floors told of hundreds of crossings. They were an orange shade of brown, worn smooth by years of bare feet, wet feet, rubbing sand.

I turned the lights back off in the living room so I could see out the large picture window. The view was utterly black. The darkness felt limitless, as if it could pull me away forever. I heard the waves; it was a distinct pleasure to hear waves from inside that house. When my eyes adjusted, I saw the white foam where the waves were crashing. They crashed mechanically; they were short, maybe two feet high, and left piles of white foam that slowly sank back, only to be pushed up and methodically dumped again, a harmless cycle.

Pressed up against the large pane of glass, I saw the whole of the room reflected behind me. And I saw the two of them. My mother bending over Megan, who was sprawled on the couch; she was pulling off Megan's wet clothes. She disentangled the small pants from Megan's feet and lifted her naked child to carry her upstairs to her bath.

The next morning I stood in the kitchen, having pulled on yesterday's clothes again. I had slept without getting any rest, without even interrupting my thoughts. At dawn I got out of bed, dressed, walked down the flight of worn steps, and brought myself to this room where the ghosts were.

The kitchen had green linoleum, shiny and bumpy like the back of a turtle. The edges of it curled up along the walls. I felt the waxy texture with my feet. I sat on one of the wooden kitchen chairs and gazed down at my feet, my toes gripping the turtle's back as though it were running away from me. I dared not look up at the surrounding walls, the room that was familiar and remembered.

Without looking, I saw the stove, its surface smoking with burned pancake batter. I saw the glass measuring cup full of batter we took turns stirring, the frying pan. I smelled the delicious smell of butter alone in a hot pan. I saw Megan's face, her tongue lodged in the corner of her mouth, her eyes slightly crossing as she lifted the glass pitcher of batter, her arms trembling with the weight of it. Determined, she tried again to make a rabbit shape.

I was the hare that ran fast. Out of this house, across the country any number of times, to doctor appointments and birthday parties, through first days of school and all the last days and ceremonies, and most heroically into adulthood. Megan was the tortoise still here in this airtight, sun-filled, seaside room.

On that first morning, I walked alongside the main road. It was narrow, with no shoulder, and the cars sped past me. I walked with my head down toward the town. Round-trip, I suppose it was a long walk, but it wasn't something I had decided to do. I walked.

When I hit the town, I entered a boutique. There were fish-and-turtle-covered sarongs, sundresses, beach slippers, and juvenile jewelry. I looked at all the things that didn't interest me. I looked at each item respectfully, wondering how I could value my time so little as to use it in this manner. I approached a wall with three short clothing racks, one above the other. On tiny plastic hangers were little-girl bathing suits.

Touching a blue one-piece, I could feel Megan's robust little torso inside. Out of the diminutive leg holes I saw her thighs covered in goose bumps. The back of the suit revealed a view of Megan's bare back, and for a moment I smelled her walnut-colored hair. I carried the suit around the store, pressed against my stomach, looking for women's suits, looking for a bathing suit like my mother's to hold this little one up against.

I returned to the house in the late afternoon. I took a blanket out to the beach. Folding myself up in it, I lay there curled on my side watching the ocean. I lay there until darkness came again.

At night, I fixed myself soup out of a can. After dinner, standing around in the living room, I noticed the old chess set on a shelf. I took down the case and removed the polished wood pieces. My mother taught me chess with this set. She and my father probably played hundreds of games with it. I set up the board on the coffee table in the living room. It started off innocently. I moved the pawns forward, the board in front of me sideways, playing each side equally. Then as the major pieces started moving, I knew that the white was Megan, and my mother also, and the black was Adrea and me. The knights had always been my favorite pieces, and I protected them most carefully. I usually lost a bishop first; I couldn't keep track of the opposing bishops and their diagonal course. A bishop took a bishop.

When I played against myself, it could be a form of meditation. In order for the game to be of any integrity, I really couldn't think of either hand's strategy. I had to keep my mind extremely empty, one move at a time. Or I could think of something else entirely. I couldn't try to make white or black win, I had to be fair. I lost a black knight. The game moved quickly, part of it was not to think too long, to just rush into it. I had the white queen moving all over, the game was going fast, and she took a black castle and bishop in two moves. But I slowed down to a stop when I saw I had left her one up and three over from my remaining black knight. I took the white queen out of the game slowly. Then I played the rest of the game, actually switching seats to view the board from behind each side. It was very important that I not cheat now. The game slowed, and the pieces dwindled down. I was moving both kings until I couldn't move one. To the left was a pawn, and the black queen and remaining castle came from the front and right. The white king was caught there. He didn't stand a chance; it was over for him. I lifted him gently off the board.

I put on my coat and headed down to the beach again. I trod slowly along the lip of the black water; it behaved like a lake. The moon was several days from full. I eyed the water suspiciously. How did it change so drastically? That night it swelled and fell back with such a gentle rhythm it seemed to welcome a small craft. I found myself longing to push out into it.

I crouched down and dipped the white king into the black water. The water moved around my hands and got my shoes wet. But it didn't move as an ocean moves. The white chess piece glowed luminescent out of the black water, and I let it go. It floated in front of me for many long moments. Shouldn't the sea carry it out, shouldn't it be whisked away?

The piano bar appeared eerily. I approached it as though it had been my destination when I left the house an hour earlier and walked along the shore. I dropped my shoes on the deck outside the huge window and stepped into them while peering in. A group of men stood around the piano singing and drinking. I was surprised how much I felt like being around people in that welcoming, lit-up space. Hesitant, I stood in the dark outside, looking into the brightness. A couple emerged and drunkenly told me, "Go

in girl, you may be the only one, but girls are allowed."
They laughed and drifted down to the beach.

I squeezed my way around the singers and took a stool
by the bar. I sipped a bourbon and watched the heartwarming
performance. There's great camaraderie in a piano bar.
They were singing a show tune, jovial and familiar. Perhaps
we all shared something in common; although not all the
same age, we'd all grown up with that music. It may have
been a particular type of family that each of us came from,
families who listened to musicals. Three men stood together,
their arms around each other, singing. I felt affection
for each singer, enjoying himself for the moment. We
must take these moments of pleasure and warmth. Take
them, I thought, this is how we endure.

~

About a week after Megan died, I was awakened in my bed by
my mother's touch. She sat on the edge of my bed, leaning
over me, stroking my hair back from my forehead. It seemed
that she wanted to wake me. When I opened my eyes, she
smiled at me and continued to stroke my head. My eyelids
opened and fell. It was hours before our normal waking time.
Her voice brought me fully awake. She assertively asked if I
was hungry. Knowing she wanted me to be, I said yes.

She left the room and returned with a white bowl, a
spoon sticking out. She sat purposefully on the side of my
bed and spoon-fed me applesauce. I swallowed each
mouthful anxiously. I closed my eyes so I wouldn't cry and
continued opening my mouth for her. When I'd finished
the bowl she said, "Good baby," and left the room. I was
eight years old.

"Tonight—you know . . . don't come."
"I won't leave you."
"It'll look as if I'm suffering. It'll look a little as if I'm

dying. It'll look that way. Do not come to see that; it's not worth the trouble."

"I won't leave you."

The little prince wanted to see the world. He left his prince-sized planet to explore foreign lands. From birth to death are we much different? We come into this world with our personhood already about us. We are each princes with something unique to share with our planet. And sometimes very quickly, like the little prince, we've had enough. We know the worth and vulnerability of the place from which we came and that it is time to go home. I have said that Adrea is like the little prince. But she isn't, Megan was. He reminded me of Megan, whimsical and lofty, and made short for this world. Rushing back and disappearing into the place from where she came.

The only way for the little prince to go home was death, and to make that choice meant suicide.

"Ah, you're here. You were wrong to come. You'll suffer. I'll look as if I'm dead; and that won't be true . . ."

I said nothing.

"You understand. It's too far. I can't take this body with me. It's too heavy."

I said nothing.

"But it'll be like an old abandoned shell. There's nothing sad about an old shell . . ."

I thought of my good-bye with Adrea two days earlier. She was happy to be staying home with Pablo, she didn't mind that I'd be gone for a weekend. She looked through the small duffel bag I'd packed and put in a chocolate bar from the kitchen. She looked over my shoulder while I found a rental car online, signing, "Get a red one, a convertible, it's fun!" And then strangely cognizant of the importance of my trip, she said. "Maybe you should take some of those pictures of Megan to leave with the house."

I was silent for a moment, in surprise, and then said, "Thanks, Adrea, that's a very good idea."

I had brought a photo of Megan seated in my mother's lap taken in this house. I tucked it under the lining in the dresser drawer in the bedroom where I was sleeping. Who knew where the dresser would end up, or who would be the next people to inhabit these rooms, but my mother and sister's image would reside here for now. I prepared the house for my departure. I notified the ghosts that I would be going home. I found Megan in the living room, flopped in a rocking chair, legs and arms spread out like a rag doll's. She was exhausted by a day on the beach. She still wore her suit and hadn't been given a bath. Her skin was starting to chill, but no adult had told her she must do anything. She might go to sleep with sand stuck in the folds of her skin and tar on her feet. If she drifted off to sleep before the adults made dinner, she would be woken and fed. But usually she urged the dinner along with her demands of hunger. Tonight she was wiped out and would rather sit and rock herself than get involved with the adults.

The ghost did not recognize me. If my own eight-year-old "ghost" were also in the house, my sister's ghost would have a question for her. "Anna, can you make me a cat's cradle? Have you ever found a genie in a magic bottle?"

But instead I told her, "Megan, I am your sister, all grown up, and I have a little girl. I came to say good-bye to you." She furrowed her eyebrows together for an instant and looked away. This was nonsense I was telling her, and she was only waiting for dinner and might perhaps put on her pajamas herself, since she was cold and no one was suggesting it.

The bedrooms, which I found without ghosts, I tidied,

and closed the doors as though new guests would be arriving. I wanted to leave it that way.

Eventually I came across my mother. She was standing at the bottom of the stairway, leaning impatiently, ready to be running, fetching something, her camera, journal, marijuana, sweater, wineglass, bathing suit, crying child, and she was listening to someone calling to her. The someone was my father, and I could hear him too, from the kitchen, telling her the end of something, not a request or instruction, but an idea.

That was what they did before their child died.

They spoke incessantly. They exchanged thoughts on all subjects. They challenged and agreed or debated. They told long stories and shared philosophies they had not known about each other. They forgot to feed the children. They played music at high volume. They never worried about waking anyone or when to sleep themselves. They drank and smoked. They ate whenever they felt like it. They read and wrote as if it were important to the world. They played with their kids and other people's kids. They played games with each other and with us.

I was not recognizable to my mother either. I was just a strange woman approaching her on the stairs. For this I received a beautiful smile. I said to her, "Do you think I look like Anna? I'm her, grown-up. I loved you very much, and I still do."

I did not give her any of the bad news. She put her arm around my shoulder and kissed my cheek. It didn't make any sense, but it may not have been impossible. She called back to her husband. I said that I was leaving.

"Safe travels," and another phenomenal smile.

There was nothing but a yellow flash close to his ankle. He remained motionless for an instant. He didn't cry out. He fell gently, the way a tree falls. There wasn't even a sound, because of the sand.

On my last night on the Cape, I walked along the beach. The light had escaped the day, but in its hurry it left shreds of itself in the darkening sky. As I walked the shoreline, a strange peace came over me. The rest of the world seemed held at bay. The hills lay where they ought to. The animal kingdom roamed or slept, inevitably killed or died in their way. The people in cities and villages each had their task and their meaning and were all right. For this moment all things were well placed.

I stopped walking and looked hard at the ocean. I saw my younger self standing on the shore, my legs planted, feet gripping the sand. I recalled the ragged feeling of my breath in my throat, my fingernails digging into my cheeks. And something else that was important to remember. I had been holding my breath, willing Megan to return with all my might. I have always felt that I didn't try to save her, that I did nothing. I was eight years old, I thought, as old as Adrea is now. I couldn't have saved Megan, I was only a child.

I stripped off my clothes and entered the waves. I swam out far beyond the breaks and treaded water. I breathed through the cold, my body growing numb. Above me, the night sky was layered; the top was dark and blue, hung with stars like muted balls of light. Beneath this layer, the sky was darker, black softened by fog. The lowest portion of the sky sat on the ocean, violet, seemingly within arm's reach. I thought it might have been reflected lights from town or because the moon was full and near. I floated in this violet nightfall.

I emerged from the water, rubbed myself with my clothes, and put them back on. The ocean was clearly different tonight; it was alive and churning as if it were trying to tell me something. I stood on the shore trying to listen. The water on the surface of the ocean sloshed around in disordered patterns, turbulent from the motion below. And in the concave dunes between the caps were blue puddles of light.

All the living souls within the ocean were making a fuss of themselves. Legions of whales, sea lions, porpoises, stingrays, turtles, fish, and plankton were awake and making their way in the depths. They had the good fortune to live where man could not.

The air was charged. I turned toward home. As my feet crashed in the shallow water, bright white sparks were thrown off under each step. Were these little microscopic creatures being killed? Or just alerting each other to two large pale intruders? I didn't slow or hesitate in my steps; I walked as fast and hard as I walk the city street at night. I was mystified by these magical fluorescent lights shooting from beneath my feet.

Before Megan died, my mother often drew our attention to these minor miracles, wanting us to see that the beauty of life is in the natural world: in every animal and plant, mountain and stone, the sky, the sea, and in us humans too. All of it is susceptible to the changing tides, fleeting and lasting both.

As a child I believed that there was magic in my hands. I would clap them together so fast that they sang, that they made a new shape, that they threw sparks.

Acknowledgments

I owe much gratitude to Susan Herman for "godmothering" this book on its way. My agent, Joëlle Delbourgo is talented and brave, believing in this project and in her own ability. Emily Bower, my editor, read this manuscript with uncanny astuteness and worked on it with steady concentration. And thanks to Chloe Foster and Steven Pomije at Trumpeter, who have made me feel I'm in good hands. I'd also like to thank my teachers at the American Sign Language Institute in Manhattan as well as the deaf staff and members of Fountain House for guiding my learning of ASL and about Deaf culture. Many faculty members at Sarah Lawrence College helped with the original manuscript, especially Suzanne Gardinier, Mary LaChapelle, and Lucy Rosenthal. My writing group, the Exiles, deserve much thanks—great writers and editors all. I thank the Faulkner House for the great literary spirit of their annual conference; the William Faulkner-William Wisdom Creative Writing Competition gave this book a new little engine. I am thankful to Antoine de Saint-Exupéry for the journey every time I look for it and the little prince for being a beloved guide. I am forever appreciative of my entire family, especially my parents, Richard and Marilyn for their encouragement and shared excitement. Lastly, much thanks and love to Bill Gullo, my generous reader, who inspires me everyday by his example.

Credits